CALL OF THE DEAD

The Ghost Reapers Series
BOOK 1

IAN FORTEY
AND
RON RIPLEY

EDITED BY ANNE LAO
AND DAWN KLEMISH

ISBN: 979-8-89476-275-3
Copyright © 2024 by ScareStreet.com

ENTER THE REALM OF TERROR...

We'd like to take a moment to thank you for your support and invite you to join our VIP newsletter.

Dive deeper into the darkness with exclusive offers, early access to new releases, and bone-chilling deals when you sign up at www.ScareStreet.com.

Let the nightmares begin…

See you in the shadows,
Scare Street

PROLOGUE

Cicadas trilled in trees, enticed by the light of the moon to share their song. The night was hot, too hot for the time of year, and the country was at the peak of an unprecedented heatwave. It made people miserable and distracted. Distracted people made mistakes.

Spotlights placed at regular intervals along the fence competed with the moon to flood the darkness with silver-white light. Each was posted near a tangle of security cameras that were pointed in every conceivable direction. The compound sought to ensure no one could approach unseen.

Armed guards were on staggered patrols in teams of two. They followed a standard sweep that changed every thirty minutes and allowed teams to swap positions in a counterclockwise pattern around the base. The idea was that no one would get too distracted or too comfortable. Fresh eyes and a fresh landscape every thirty minutes.

Gate security did not swap out, though. A four-man team monitored the guard station, checking vehicles as they passed in and out. They remained on an eight-hour shift and kept in radio contact with the security office inside.

The setup was efficient and well-run. The guards seemed well-trained. No one paused for cigarette breaks, and no one left their post for a nap or even a bathroom break. They had discipline. But it would not be enough.

It was just past two in the morning. A truck, unmarked with tinted windows, rolled up to the security gate the same way it had done three times a week for months. The guards went about the process of verifying the driver's credentials.

Six figures in black rushed to the eastern fence, avoiding the sweep of the spotlights. The nearest light always focused on the gate when the truck came. They had two minutes and fifteen seconds.

Links in the fence snapped with a muffled, metallic clink. The bolt cutters chewed through them with ease, two pairs working simultaneously until they met in the center. The lead man pushed the fence in, and the six figures passed through the perimeter and onto the grounds undetected.

The truck entered the compound, driving up the long road to the central building. The two minutes and fifteen seconds were up. The spotlight swung back, away from the gate and toward the perimeter fence. The bright, white beam illuminated the grass and dirt and weeds as it came toward the six, black-clad figures. And then it died.

Inside the tower, the guard puzzled over the light, checking the controls and power line. The six figures on the ground continued toward the building.

✳ ✳ ✳

"East tower one light is down," the man at the security station said to no one in particular. His supervisor was in the room somewhere, but he did not turn his head from the computer. Instead, he scrolled through a series of updates.

"We've lost cameras sixteen, seventeen, eighteen, twenty-two, twenty-three, and twenty-four as well."

Six stations monitored facility security, two external and four internal. Gustav Novak monitored the east and south lights and cameras. He'd had the job for six years and had helped stop three break-ins and some petty vandalism.

"East tower two is down," Novak added.

He spoke English for the benefit of the supervisor, but his Czech accent was unmistakable. Most of the employees were Czech, Slovak, Bulgarian, or Serbian. There were a few Germans in maintenance, and

Russians worked in the lab. But the big bosses were British and American.

"How can two lights and six cameras just go down?" Mr. Harper, Novak's supervisor, asked as he appeared behind the station.

"Unknown, sir. No reports from the guards."

Three more cameras dropped from the feed, and three more lights shorted out as well.

"East One, this is Central. What's happening out there?" Harper asked over the radio. There was a pause before the radio crackled in response.

"Everything died. I've got no power on the tower at all," came the reply from the guard.

"East Two?" Harper asked.

"Same," came the reply. "Nothing's working. Varga has gone down to check the box."

Harper lowered the radio and looked at Novak's monitor.

"Nothing else is down?"

"No, sir," Novak answered. On a whim, he switched his panel from an itemized list to the map view of the compound.

"*Sakra*," Novak muttered, slipping into his native language.

"Jesus," Harper whispered, echoing his sentiment.

On the map view, the pattern of power outages formed a trail from the fence to the northeast corner of the building. It was too perfect to be a coincidence or any random power failure.

"Sir, this is Harper in security. I think we have a breach," he said into his radio. Novak switched camera feeds and redirected lights to the areas that had been left uncovered. More cameras died, and the lights followed.

The door to the security office opened. Novak ignored it, working on catching sight of whoever had cut off their power. Others were on their radios, raising guards and asking for updates. The usually quiet security office was now a chaotic mess of keys clicking and radio static as people talked over one another.

"Move aside," a deep voice said, pushing Novak's chair away from his station before he had a chance to respond at all.

Major Lucas Jones was a tall man with massive arms and legs and a bald head that bore scars from where shrapnel had nearly killed him some years earlier. He had served with the U.S. Army Green Berets, people said, but Novak had never confirmed that. All he knew was that Jones had no sense of humor, and if he pushed you out of his way, you simply stayed out of his way.

Keys clicked in rapid succession as Jones brought up security protocols that Novak had no access to. Camera feeds died one by one as the Major tried to access everything to get them eyes on the outside.

"Sound the general alarm. Now," Jones ordered.

One of the other station monitors reached across the control panel and slapped his palm against the large, red button. Nothing happened.

Voices went silent. The man, Yuri, slapped the red button again and again. No alarm sounded.

Jones turned from Novak's monitor and looked at Yuri and the red button.

"Son, you care to explain why I'm not hearing an alarm right now?"

"I don't know, sir. I... I hit the button."

"You hit the button," Jones repeated quietly. He reached over and slammed his fist down on it. All the monitors in the office went dead, along with the lights.

Red backup lights clicked to life, bathing the room in a bloody glow. All the computers were out. Jones took the radio from Harper's hand.

"This is Major Jones. All teams converge on Central."

The radio clicked with a faint static hiss. The men in the room all but held their breath as they waited for the reply. Novak watched the radio in the big man's hand.

"This is Major Jones. All teams converge on Central. Confirm," he repeated.

The faint static hiss ended quickly. No one replied.

"All teams report positions immediately," Jones ordered.

No answer was forthcoming. The major pushed the radio against Harper's chest, forcing the other man to take it.

"The base has been compromised. Arm yourselves," Jones ordered.

Novak stood frozen for a moment. He heard the order, but it had not fully clicked in his brain. He was a security officer only in the most technical sense. He worked on computers. He was not trained to fight people. He was not a soldier.

"Novak, move," Harper said.

Others had unlocked the weapons locker and removed the sidearms: One CZ 75 semiautomatic pistol for each team member, and a spare ammunition clip. No one had ever taught Novak how to use it.

Jones had already drawn his weapon. It was a larger gun than the ones used by base security, and silver instead of black. It made Novak think of American movies. Jones was some kind of modern-day cowboy with his massive gun and scarred head. Novak did not doubt that Jones knew how to use his weapon.

"They're coming for that door," Jones said, pointing to the far side of the room. "You will not let them pass."

Novak looked at the door. It had no window and no sign on it. Access was through a security keypad. It had never been opened in Novak's presence, nor had anyone told him what was on the other side.

It was what they were guarding in the facility, however.

If it was something they made or something they found, Novak didn't know. It could have been a trillion dollars in gold, a nuclear weapon, or even an alien spaceship. His job was not to know, just to keep it safe.

Somewhere in the building, someone screamed. Gunfire, muffled by the walls, filled the silence that followed. The men in the room took up positions focused on the single entrance. Jones crouched low, his big movie-cop gun trained on the center of the door. Novak held his limply at his side.

More gunfire and more screams. Novak felt his pulse race and could not control his breathing. He wasn't going to panic, he told himself over and over. He would not panic. He could not.

"Hey. You want to put your guns down?" a voice yelled from outside the door. The accent was American.

"Come and make us," Jones yelled back.

Novak crouched between a monitoring station and the door that led to whatever the infiltrators were after. He took deep breaths and wiped the sweat from his brow.

"You must be Major Jones," the voice outside yelled. "I read your file. Dishonorable discharge? Tsk tsk."

Jones pulled back the hammer on his gun, his arms trained at the entrance.

"Listen, we don't have to kill anyone. You toss your guns, you come out, and everyone gets to have flapjacks come breakfast. One-time offer," the mystery man beyond the door said.

"You will not leave this place alive," Jones assured the man.

The doorknob rattled and Novak winced as gunfire exploded through the room. Jones fired at the door, and his weapon was like a cannon. One shot, two, three, five, seven. It was like thunder inside his head with every blast. He covered his ears and winced with every shot.

The bullets tore holes through the door and the frame all around the handle. There was only a moment of silence when he was finished before someone outside laughed.

"Is that a Desert Eagle?" the man asked, still laughing. "What, are you hunting 90s action movie stars?"

"Come back to the door and find out," Jones hissed.

The man outside laughed again.

"Oh, Major. You're a treat. But I told you my offer was a one-time thing. I can't go back on my word in front of my men now, can I? Your time's up."

"We'll see whose time is up," Jones yelled.

From his hiding place, Novak could only watch and feel his stomach tighten into knots. He didn't want to die for a job. He didn't care what was in the room or who the men who wanted it were. It was not his fight. And yet, he was still in the thick of it.

The sweat on his brow grew cold. The red emergency lights flickered, and he thought for a moment that the intruders had somehow cut the backup generators. And then he saw something new.

A man was in the room who had not been there before. He was between Novak and Jones. The major, with his back to the newcomer, had no idea.

The new arrival was tall and thin. Too thin, in fact. He was naked, his flesh pale even in the red lights, and Novak could count every rib and vertebra along the man's back.

It was as though the muscles of the stranger's body had been eaten away and all that remained was flesh pulled tightly on bone. Thin, dark hair hung in wispy clumps from the man's head. Novak could not see his face. He was stricken with such terror at seeing even the shape of the man that he did not want to.

The skeletal man made no sound. His hands were on Jones' throat for a moment, not even a heartbeat, and then the major's head pulled from his body. Someone shouted and guns fired. Bullets ricocheted off walls and shattered computers. The skeletal man was unaffected. Nothing hit him. Nothing stopped him. He swung long, thin arms from man to man, slicing throats with curved, ragged fingernails.

Novak held his eyes shut. Even after the gunfire ceased, he kept them squeezed shut as tightly as he could, tears streaming down his cheeks. His breath came in shudders, and he did not even know where his gun was.

"Open your eyes," a voice whispered, wet, and strained. Novak shook his head, but hands like ice encircled his face and held him still. "Open

7

your eyes."

He opened his eyes. The last thing he heard before he died was his own screams.

CHAPTER 1
FROM THE PAST

"I'm gonna have to cut you off before you float away, hun."

Shane Ryan looked up at the woman holding the pot of coffee and raised an eyebrow. She was in her fifties, and her brown and gray hair was held in a big braid at the back of her head. She smiled warmly.

"This is your fifth coffee. You're gonna be high on caffeine for the rest of the day."

"Helps me keep my edge," he told her as she refilled his mug.

"Well, as long as you're not too jittery," she replied. "Let me know if you change your mind about breakfast."

"Will do," he said. "Thank you."

Five coffees and two pieces of plain toast was not a breakfast special at the Temple Street Diner, and his server had been trying hard to sell him on the "make your own omelet" deal.

He'd just returned to town after being in Nevada cleaning up after a desert spirit that had a taste for tourists. He was just looking to relax. Maybe five cups of coffee wasn't relaxing for some, but it was what he needed. He was glad to be back in Nashua. Home shouldn't be a vacation, he thought, but it was starting to feel that way.

He stared out the diner window, past the cars in the parking lot and those passing on the street. He'd seen three ghosts on his way to the diner from his home. One was walking like any other pedestrian, one was sitting on a lawn, and one was in the middle of traffic, still like a statue. There was nowhere to go to escape them. They were everywhere.

His eyes drifted across the diner. On the far side, on one of the barstool seats that faced the kitchen, was another ghost. This one was a young man, maybe in his mid-twenties. His face was half burned, almost down to the bone. He'd arrived about ten minutes earlier.

He was just sitting there as though waiting for an order. Shane didn't bother focusing on him too long. He didn't want to give away that he could see him at all, lest the spirit decide to come over to chat.

The bell over the diner door jingled, and a man entered. Shane's eyes were back toward the window and the world outside. Green grass, blue skies. It looked like a peaceful day. A good day to be back home.

"Well, I will be damned."

The man who had just entered sat in the booth opposite Shane. The men looked at each other, Shane focusing on the stranger's face for the first time. The dark hair, the scarred chin, the heavy gray eyes. It was older than Shane remembered, but of course it would be.

"Blakely," Shane said.

"Shane Ryan, as I live and breathe, you look like you've aged a hundred years."

Davis Blakely laughed and held out a hand across the table. The last time Shane had seen Blakely, they were stationed in some backwater corner of a desert where supply runs were about as common as unicorns and communications were even worse.

He took the other man's hand and they both half-stood, leaning awkwardly across the table. Blakely threw an arm around Shane's shoulders, patting him on the back and laughing.

"What are you doing here? How did you even find me?" Shane asked as they sat again.

Blakely's grin was as wide as ever.

"How did I find you? You're predictable as hell. Coffee and toast, just like always," Blakely said, nodding to his breakfast. "And I'm here to see you, man! Can't a guy look up an old friend?"

"You out now?" Shane asked.

He was not dressed like a soldier. He wore a suit, and an expensive one at that. But Shane clocked the sidearm under his jacket the moment he approached. Blakely shrugged, half demure.

"Never really out, are we? Once a Marine, always a Marine."

"Always," Shane agreed.

"But retired? Yeah. Couple of years now."

"Retired to Nashua?"

Blakely laughed and shook his head.

"Hell, no. No offense, brother, but this place is so dead, I'm surprised no one's buried it yet."

"Just the way I like it." Shane sipped his coffee.

"Yeah? You gave up on chasing that high? Following the action? I remember you in the thick of it; you can't tell me there wasn't a thrill there."

"Oh, for sure. Nothing like people shooting at you to make you feel alive." Shane grinned.

Shane never thought Blakely was crazy like some of the other guys did. It was just how he dealt with stress. Some guys got angry, some prayed, and Blakely laughed. Laughed and dodged bullets. Even under enemy fire, he was a Marine whose enjoyment of chaos could never be tempered. Everything amused Blakely, no matter how grim. But he'd pulled Shane's ass out of the fire more than once, and he'd returned the favor.

"So, what happened, man? What do you do now?"

"Retired," Shane said. "I drink coffee. I read. I translate documents sometimes."

Blakely scoffed.

"Man, you are full of it. I know you're doing some kind of work. I saw that house of yours. It's like the Addams Family mansion; that thing can't be cheap."

"Family home," Shane pointed out. "You stopped by?"

"Was looking for you, yeah." Blakely nodded. "I took up a new gig a while back. Consulting. I'm usually overseas, but I'm stateside for a few days and was nearby, so…"

"So, you stalked me and followed me to a diner? That tracks," Shane said.

His old friend laughed.

"Like I said, I'm in military consulting. Had to look you up because I've got a new job coming up, and I was thinking of bringing you in on it. You know, if you're interested."

Shane took another sip of his coffee and leveled Blakely with an expressionless stare.

"You came to the United States in that suit to offer me a job doing consulting?"

"You're such an ass," Blakely said, shaking his head and laughing. "This suit is worth more than that ugly-ass car you drive. But yes, I did. I remember my friends. I work with a couple of the guys from our old unit, Luther Washington and Penn Leclerc."

"That bodes well," Shane joked. He barely remembered Washington, but Leclerc was unpleasant in general.

"Seriously, Ryan, this is the real deal. The money I'm making? You wouldn't believe it. And for a guy like you, this work would be a walk in the park."

Shane nodded. The shift in tone from his old friend was palpable. Joker though he was, Blakely had his serious side.

"What does 'consulting' mean these days?" Shane asked.

"We do security assessments, asset acquisitions, risk management, reconnaissance, cyber security, you name it. It's taking what the Corps taught us and using it for ourselves. You could be making seven figures, easy."

"But for who?" Shane asked. "Who gets the recon run on them? What assets are you acquiring?"

Blakely smiled wider than ever.

"C'mon, man. You know how this works. I'm already telling you more than I should. You come in with me, sign on to the team, and you get on the need-to-know list."

Shane exhaled loudly and lifted his mug.

"Good thing you didn't retire to sales because you are not selling this one at all."

"I wouldn't be here if this wasn't the real deal, Ryan. I want guys I know with me, guys I trust. I'm doing good now, but with you and some of the other guys? This could be great. It's legit work, man."

"Yeah, but private military contractors? Blakely, come on," Shane said.

Blakely shook his head.

"We're consultants, Ryan. We're not out there putting civilians at risk. We curate our clients carefully. We have to. Trust me, the jobs we take, they're for the greater good. We're making a difference, even if no one knows it. And we're making money. We're earning what we're worth. Don't tell me you never felt like you should be getting what you were owed."

"Now you're selling something," Shane said. "Your next job must be a kicker."

"It's not like that. It's me!" Blakely said, feigning indignance. "You know me better than that."

In truth, Shane did not know Blakely that well. He trusted him with his life, and Blakely had done the same. That had made them brothers. But years had passed since then. Shane had no idea who the man was now. But he knew what military contractors did.

"So, what are we talking about? You're not working stateside, so where are you right now? Ukraine? Afghanistan?"

"We're overseas," Blakely said, being happily evasive in his answer. "It's not face-down in the mud or choking on sand in the desert. I have an office. I have a bar with cognac right next to the computer, and beer in the fridge. It's a solid gig."

"Sounds like you've made it. If you have a company and you're making money, I don't know that I can bring anything to the table."

"Come off it," Blakely said. "Like I said, I want people I know and trust in on this."

"Meaning you don't trust the guys who are in on it now."

It was the first time the illusion of Blakely's happiness seemed to crack. He shook his head, tapping absently on the table.

"Not like that, no. The team is good. Solid. You know how it is, though. If you're going into the thick of it, you'd rather have guys who've bled and sweated with you in the past watching your back."

"Sounds like intense consulting."

Blakely wasn't saying the obvious because he didn't want to. But he knew Shane would get what he was talking about. Expertly curated clientele or not, Blakely was doing mercenary work. He was soldiering for profit. It wasn't illegal; plenty of firms did the same thing. But it was high-risk, and there were gray zones when it came to laws and ethics. It wasn't a ride Shane was looking to take. He'd done his duty and put it behind him. That life was in the past.

"You have to at least consider it. Look, the company's called Silvershore Corporation. Take my card, at least. Give me a call sometime. Hell, just to talk, man. Shouldn't have taken me stalking you to New Hampshire for us to keep in touch."

He slid a simple business card across the table. The name "Silvershore" was printed in bold, silver letters above a phone number on thick, smooth card stock. There was no name on it.

"Fancy," Shane said, eyeing the card before slipping it into his pocket.

"You have no idea," Blakely said, nodding. "I'm telling you, it's a whole different world. You could afford some hair plugs, a couple of new fingers, improve your overall look."

"Oh, fingers, huh?" Shane said. "I really only ever need this." He raised his middle finger at the other man.

Blakely laughed and shook his head.

"Listen, I'm not even supposed to be in New Hampshire. I have to get to New York and then I'm back on a plane in a few hours, but I wanted to come and talk to you in person. Please, no joke. Think about it, okay? It's good money, Ryan. Good money for work you could do in your sleep."

"I'll think about it," Shane promised.

His friend stood up, and Shane did the same. They stepped away from the table and shook hands. Blakely pulled Shane close, embracing him while their hands were still clasped.

"It's good to see you again, man. It really is."

"Yeah," Shane agreed, clapping the other man on the back.

"I'm expecting your call," his friend replied as they parted. "Don't leave me hanging on this one."

Blakely left and Shane watched him head out to a black sedan in the parking lot. A moment after he pulled out of the driveway, the ghost by the bar left as well, and Shane watched him drift through the glass door out to the parking lot, and then vanish from sight.

CHAPTER 2

IN A STRANGE LAND

Shane had set his phone on the table in the kitchen. He ran his hands across his face slowly, letting out a long sigh.

"Is something wrong?"

The voice was cheerful and inquisitive, and Shane lowered his hands to look at Eloise. The ghost of the little girl was sitting in the chair opposite his. The bows in her hair looked redder than usual today somehow, a contrast to the old and discolored dress and flesh of her ghostly form.

"Unexpected news," he answered. The phone on the table displayed an article from a news website. Eloise leaned over and looked at it.

"U.S. military contractor dies in conflict," she read the headline.

Davis Blakely had died. It had been one week since Shane had met his old friend at the diner. Shane had not thought about Blakely's offer at all. He had no interest in that sort of work, and no interest in going overseas again.

"Where is Vakovia?" Eloise asked, reading more of the article.

"Central Europe," Carl answered, entering the room as well. "It used to have another name, but it escapes me just now. Why do you ask?"

"Someone Shane knew died there, I think," Eloise answered.

"Oh?" The German ghost looked at Shane's phone as well.

"Retired Staff Sergeant Davis Blakely, founder of the military contracting group Silvershore, was the only fatality of a clash with Vakovian militants near the country's eastern border," he read out loud.

Shane took the phone from the table and slipped it into his pocket. There were few details in the story other than it being the result of an armed conflict and Blakely being the only casualty.

"You do not often talk about your comrades in the military," Carl said. "Was this Blakely a friend?"

"I saw him last week," Shane replied. "He offered me a job."

"That is an interesting coincidence," the ghost said.

"It's something," Shane agreed. He wasn't sure it was a coincidence. "Blakely said he wanted guys he could trust on his team."

"Meaning he did not trust the men he was working with," Carl added.

"That's what I thought. I brushed him off. But now this... the timing makes me wonder."

"Did he die in battle?" Eloise asked. "Is it a war?"

"No. And no," Shane answered. "He said he's a consultant. But his company is a military contractor. Sounded like standard mercenary stuff to me."

"A private army," Carl said.

"Not an army. But a unit, sure. Highly trained retired military. Probably all Marines, SEALs, Rangers, that sort of thing."

Carl raised an eyebrow. "Men trained to work as a team and to kill."

Shane grunted. He never thought Blakely was the kind of guy to do some of the darker stuff mercs might get wrapped up in. Assassination jobs, or "urban pacification" as they called it. He didn't think he was out there killing people. But people got caught in the crossfire with these kinds of groups, and a soldier motivated by money was sometimes fast on the trigger.

The story said he'd been killed by militants. Shane didn't know what Vakovian militants were doing, what they wanted, or what Silvershore might have wanted with them. But for Blakely to be the only casualty was strange. Why would he have been in a position to get into a firefight that sounded like a border skirmish?

"This death troubles you." Carl stood at the edge of the table and watched Shane, his hands clutched behind his back.

"Smells funny," Shane explained. "Coming to me about a job—this job—and then dying. No one else is lost. No more details provided. *Something* happened out there."

"Surely the local law enforcement will look into it," Carl suggested.

"Maybe." Shane shrugged. "But there was a ghost at the diner where I met Davis. Arrived a few minutes before him and left right after. At the time, I didn't think much of it, but after it left, it got me wondering."

"You think a ghost was after your friend?" Eloise asked.

"No. I think the ghost was with him. He was only in Nashua to see me, just for a few minutes. I think Davis brought it with him."

"He could see spirits as well?" Carl asked.

"Never came up when we served. But it's not unprecedented for someone in his line of work. The Endless Night had ghost mercs."

"I recall," Carl said, making a face. "So, you think your friend knew about your abilities?"

"Maybe. He said he'd seen the house. The ghost was in the diner for some time before Davis appeared. He might have been tailing me for a while. Must have done some research. If he's connected like that, my name could have come up."

"Then his death might be related to the ghost," Carl offered.

"Or other ghosts. He was doing something over there that had him on edge enough to want to shake up his team."

"Are you going away again, Shane Ryan?" Eloise asked, a hint of stern disapproval in her voice.

Shane could think of nothing he wanted to do less than fly across the ocean to a central European nation amid a bubbling civil war. He knew little of Vakovian politics beyond what showed up in the news, and that was enough to know he should stay out of it. But that didn't change the fact that Davis Blakely was dead.

"Maybe."

"You just got back!" the young ghost cried. "This is highly

irresponsible behavior. The house doesn't run itself, you know."

"It does, actually," Carl countered.

"Not helpful," Eloise shot back. "We're your friends, too. What about us?"

"Blakely saved my life," Shane said simply. "Pulled me out of the way of an IED and got a shoulder full of shrapnel for his efforts. He was a joker, and he needed to take things more seriously, but he was a good man. A good Marine. And he was my friend."

Carl nodded, shooting a glance at Eloise to keep her quiet.

"Then you owe it to your friend to discover the true nature of his death."

"I disagree," Eloise said angrily. "How much of a friend was he? I never met him. I know Francis and Tom. I never knew this Blakely."

"He was a friend from long ago, Eloise."

"Sometimes a friend can go away for years, and then you pick right up where you left off," Herbert added.

Shane turned around, surprised by the big ghost's presence. He didn't know how long the one-armed giant had been standing behind him.

"This is turning into a real round-table discussion," Shane said. "Anyone else want to join in? Daisy? Thaddeus?"

"I think you should go," Thaddeus answered. He was behind Herbert in the doorway, looking small and unassuming in the wake of the four-hundred-pound ghost.

Shane glanced at Carl, who only offered a slight shrug and a tight smile. Shane was not polling for opinions. He needed to find out more about what happened.

The ghosts remained behind as Shane made his way from the kitchen to the rear of the house and out into the garden. He had looked up the number for Luther Washington after learning Blakely had died.

Shane had never been friends with Penn Leclerc and had no interest in speaking to the man about what happened if he didn't have to. But

Washington had always been a decent soldier. He was young when Shane knew him, untested and a little naïve, but that changed with time as it did for everyone.

Washington was quieter than Blakely, and he liked to read, Shane remembered. He wasn't above socializing when he had the chance, but he never made himself the center of attention. Shane remembered him talking about his family a lot. Big family, spread across several states, with plenty of siblings, cousins, nieces, and nephews. He was used to taking the backseat in a crowd.

The phone rang until something clicked and the line went dead. No voicemail, just a dropped call. Shane grunted and hung up. He stood in the yard for a long moment, breathing the fresh air and watching the clouds in the distant sky.

His phone rang. The number was private. He debated answering and then lifted the handset to his ear.

"Who is this?" a man's voice asked.

"You called me," Shane pointed out.

"You called first. I called back."

"Luther?" Shane said. Silence on the other end. "Luther Washington?"

"Who is this?" the voice said again. It was quiet, as though trying not to be overheard. He sounded very stressed.

"Shane Ryan."

"Jesus," the voice said. "Shane Ryan, wow. It's been… yeah. I mean, yes, sir. This is Luther Washington."

"Don't call me sir, Luther."

"Sorry, sir. I mean, sorry, Shane. I didn't expect to hear from you."

"Didn't expect to be calling, either, but Davis stopped by last week. Offered me a job. He said you work with him now. Some military consulting firm."

"Davis." There was a long pause on Luther's end.

"What happened, Luther? News here said he was killed by militants."

"Yeah," Luther replied. "That's what they said here, too."

There was sarcasm in the way the man spoke. Anger, even. But nervousness as well. It sounded to Shane like the man was moving while he talked. Walking somewhere and doing so quickly.

"So, what happened?"

"I wasn't there."

"So, it could have been what they say?"

Another long pause answered him. He could hear Luther's breathing, fast and muffled by something.

"I can't talk about much, Shane. Not on the phone. Not now."

"No?" Shane said. "You got ears?"

"I got a lot of things," Luther replied, meaning he thought people were not just spying on him but tailing him as well. If his phone line was compromised, Shane would get no direct answers.

"What can you tell me?"

"I can tell you it's a good thing you didn't accept that job offer," the other man replied.

"What are you guys doing over there, Luther?"

There was another long period of silence and then a muffled banging sound followed by someone else's voice. The words were lost, reduced to an unintelligible drone.

"It was good talking to you again, sir. I'm sorry I can't help you."

The phone clicked, and the line went dead.

Shane stayed where he was in the yard, phone still in hand. He booked his flight to Vakovia before returning to the house.

CHAPTER 3
STRANGER

The flight out of Boston was supposed to take twelve hours with a stopover in Frankfurt. Shane had not mentioned to Carl that he'd be spending an hour in Germany, which ended up being five hours. If nothing else, his German came in handy when trying to buy cigarettes at the airport.

When he finally touched down in the Vakovian capital of Ravjek, it was noon the next day and his internal clock was off by at least eight hours. He would have no time to adjust. He wanted to get in and out of the country as quickly as he could.

His return flight was booked for five days later, with an option to extend his stay if need be. He hoped he wouldn't need the extra time.

Vakovian customs barely gave his passport a second glance after seeing he was American. The heavily armed men wandered the small, utilitarian airport in full tactical gear with at least three weapons visible, including two handguns and an assault rifle each. The airport looked like it was ready for war.

Shane made his way past customs to the front entrance and a small taxi stand. The place was crowded with cars that must have been forty years old alongside the odd sports car that would have cost more money than most people in America made in a year. It was a strange contrast, seeing the exceptional wealth and lack thereof so close together the moment he entered the city.

Ravjek was an old city, dating back to sometime in the twelfth century. It had changed its name more times than Shane could count and had been ruled by several empires in its history. Now, it was a free and allegedly democratic state with rumors of autocracy and political oppression from the ruling party. Elections had gone the way of the current president for more than twenty years, and international watchdog groups had pointed out that, in some districts, voter turnout was more than one hundred percent.

Corruption was rampant, and the poorest Vakovians were exceptionally poor while the richest were exceptionally rich. The disparity was stunning, but it made fertile ground for groups like Silvershore. High-powered, rich clients who wanted to stay rich and powerful could outsource their dirty work to mercenaries and call it all terrorism or insurgency.

Shane didn't want to think Blakely was that kind of soldier. In fact, he knew he wasn't. But that was back then. If that was what he had gotten involved in, then his death could have had any number of reasons.

A short man with a receding hairline wearing cargo shorts and a polo shirt promised Shane the cheapest cab ride to whatever his destination might be. Two other cabbies cursed them out as Shane got into the back of the man's squat, banana-yellow taxi and was greeted by the overwhelming smell of pine air freshener.

"Where do we go, good buddy?" the man asked in a thick Hungarian accent.

"Cheapest hotel you can find," Shane said. The man smiled and nodded into the rearview mirror.

"Best hotel, I know them all," he told Shane, his English serviceable enough.

"Just cheapest," Shane said. The cabbie nodded again.

"Good deal. I know the place. Best deal. It's not..." he seemed to struggle for a word.

"Clean?" Shane asked.

"Safest?" the man countered. Shane grinned.

"That's fine."

The cab lurched into motion, the engine roaring and grinding as they headed away from the airport.

"You mind if I smoke?" the cabbie asked. Shane shook his head.

"Not at all," he said, pulling his own cigarettes out. It had been forever since he'd been able to smoke in someone else's car. It was a relief that Vakovia had not caught up with the anti-smoking movement.

Both men smoked as the car rumbled across an underpass and then toward a skyline dotted with massive, rectangular buildings that looked like upended bricks, each one identical to the next.

From the outskirts of the city and almost all the way downtown, most of Ravjek looked like it was built with only a handful of blueprints. Buildings were angular, ugly, and devoid of color. Everything was a square or a rectangle, in drab, gray hues.

Closer to the downtown area, more personality arose. Churches that must have been hundreds of years old dotted the landscape, along with equally ancient buildings that had been converted to businesses. Shane saw a massive, glass skyscraper built next to one, and the difference was jarring.

For all the people that lined the streets, pedestrians shopping in an open-air market or walking across the road with no care at all for the state of traffic, what drew Shane's attention the most was the dead. There were more ghosts in the city than he had ever seen in a populated area.

It was as though downtown Ravjek was built on a cemetery. Ghosts wandered with the living, stood on corners, loomed out of windows, and more. There were dozens of them, probably hundreds by the time the cab driver turned away from the populated area and entered a shabby, rundown part of town with less foot traffic and more ramshackle structures.

"Cheap," the cabbie said, as he rolled up on the curb in front of a building that had nothing on the outside to even indicate it was a hotel. Shane looked at the building, its exterior covered in crusty, brown stucco, and then the surrounding neighborhood. Nothing was labeled in any way, not even with numbers to show an address.

"This is a hotel?" Shane asked.

"You bet, buddy. You want cheap, I got you cheap," the driver said.

Shane got out of the cab and looked around. Two stray dogs ate something from a nearby garbage can, and a ghost in a window across the street stared at him with hollow eyes. An old man with a cane was walking in the opposite direction.

"Looks good," he said, handing the driver some money and taking his bag from the car.

"Be safe. Make sure you lock the door, yeah?" the driver advised. Shane nodded, and the car drove away.

The door to the hotel was made of wood and was warped enough that it stuck in the frame, so he had to pull hard. Once he was inside, the interior stunk heavily of incense. Dim lights lined a hallway above a red carpet. There was still no sign he was in a hotel.

Shane walked the length of the hall to another door and then entered a large room that looked like some sort of Victorian gentleman's club. Everything was rich wood tones and brass fixtures that were tarnished by age and a lack of care. A ghost sat on a threadbare antique loveseat next to a dim lamp, reading a book over the shoulder of an elderly woman.

There was a desk directly ahead, behind which a sweaty man with a round face and round glasses sat, eyes drooping, a bottle of beer damp with condensation near his hand.

"I need a room," Shane said, approaching the desk.

"Hmm?" the man muttered, rousing himself.

"A room," Shane repeated. Incense burned on a small table behind the man, multiple sticks trailing smoke into the air. The whole place was in a haze that made it almost dreamlike.

"You are American," the man said, his accent harder to place than the cabbie's.

"Yes," Shane agreed.

"And you want room?" he asked as though the concept made no sense. He squinted behind his tiny glasses.

"A room for five days and fewer questions," Shane clarified. He put a handful of American bills on the desk and the man nodded.

"Room seven. Up the stairs and left. Fresh linens in hallway. Shower is good, water hot. Make sure you lock door."

The man slid a key to Shane. He didn't ask for his name, didn't ask him to sign anything, and didn't offer any change.

"You need anything later, you call desk. Ask for Milos. Girls, drinks, party favors. You name it. Ask for Milos."

Milos didn't bother looking at Shane when he made his offer, and he didn't look like the sort of guy to trust with procuring anything, but maybe that was part of his gimmick.

"I'll keep that in mind," Shane said.

Shane followed the directions up the stairs and down the hall to room seven, the floorboards of the old building creaking underfoot with every other step. He unlocked the door and closed it behind him.

The room was small but serviceable. The floor only creaked at the door's entrance, which was a minor relief. He'd be able to hear anyone trying to make their way in if it came to that.

A window looked out over the street he'd entered from and gave him a view of the city's skyline in the distance. The ghost across the street was still in the window, staring out blankly.

Shane dropped his bag on the bed and opened one of the two doors in the room. The bathroom was cramped. There was a shower but no tub, and the tiles looked like they might have been as old as some of the city's churches.

The second door was to the closet, and Shane grunted as he pulled it open. The ghost of a middle-aged man was slumped against the wall, his flesh bloated and purple on one side. He was sitting as though he'd fallen over drunk, and Shane shook his head.

"You can't stay in here," he said.

"*Toto je moj domov*," the ghost muttered in a gurgle.

"I have no idea what that means. Go," Shane lied. He knew how chatty ghosts could get. He had no time for that.

"*Chod' do pekla*," the ghost replied.

Shane kicked the ghost in the leg, and his eyes widened.

"*Ako?*"

"Out," Shane ordered. He kicked the ghost harder, who scowled as he got to his feet awkwardly.

"*Hlupy American*," the ghost growled, shambling out of the closet. The words might not have been familiar, but the ghost's tone of voice suggested he wasn't wishing him well.

The ghost drifted through the wall, and Shane was alone. He sat on the bed for a moment, staring out the window and thinking. He had the address for Silvershore and was confident it would not be hard to find. The company maintained a front like it was a simple, everyday business. It had an office, a website, and a contact number for questions from the media or potential clients.

With no knowledge of the city, the language, or the culture, Shane had pushed himself into a corner from the outset. He was not equipped for the job he wanted to do, and honestly, he wasn't sure what job he wanted to do. He needed to find out how Blakely had died and where. He wanted the truth, even if it turned out to just be the story in the news. But in his gut, he knew that wasn't the case. There had to be more.

He left the room and locked the door, heading out into the city for the first time. He needed to get a feel for where he was relative to where he needed to be. He didn't like the unfamiliar in a situation where knowledge was going to be his best resource.

Shane walked the city streets. He returned to the busy downtown area and scoured the open-air market, watching vendors and customers alike. He noted which stalls were cluttered with goods and blocked views from the streets as well as where alleys were between boxes of produce and trucks and tables.

The market was crowded and centralized. It would be a good place to get lost, intentionally or otherwise, and he wanted to get familiar with it just in case.

After Shane had covered the market from back to front, he headed out again, making his way to the ancient churches in the heart of the oldest part of the city. Ghosts were most prominent there, many standing or sitting and doing almost nothing. Some of them wore clothes of a style Shane couldn't even place in history, and he wondered how long the spirits had been there. Some ghosts back home had haunted places for decades, and in rare cases centuries, the Vakovian spirits made him wonder if he needed to add a digit to his estimates.

He avoided direct contact with the spirits as much as he could. He was certain the oldest ones would not speak English, and many of them had an angry air about them. They watched the living with derision or outright hostility. He wondered how often hauntings in the city turned violent.

It was entering early evening when Shane's path took him toward Silvershore's office. It was not near downtown as he thought at first when he read what street it was on. Instead, the road extended from near the market for several miles into a rundown industrial part of the city that looked like a relic of the Cold War.

Factories and plants belched smoke and steam into the air, dotted across a landscape that had an equal number of ruins from buildings long since out of business. Trucks ran up and down the roads, and heaps of scrap were piled haphazardly on the roadside as though the region had been born out of an old dump.

Shane passed over dozens of railroad tracks that looked like they hadn't been used in years, many grown over with weeds. In some cases, the rails were visibly warped from the weather. Nothing looked like it had been cared for in decades.

Shane approached a series of small, lunchbox-like office buildings from across a lot next to an abandoned ironworks factory. What must have once been a monstrous production facility was now speckled with rusted heaps of metal, overgrown weeds, and trees that grew out of cracks in the empty wasteland of a parking lot.

Across from the ironworks factory, a clean but nondescript building sat next to a new, rust-free fence topped with razor wire that encircled a parking lot. The vehicles parked within were all brand-new, clean, shiny, and forgettable black SUVs with tinted windows, each nearly identical to the next.

The building was modern, mostly glass, with a simple sign on the front wall that read "Silvershore Consulting" in the same script on the business card Blakely had given Shane.

Security cameras dotted the building's exterior, pointed at the parking lot, the entrance, and elsewhere, giving full coverage to every side of the building. There was noticeable comms equipment on the roof.

Shane stopped in the ironworks lot, keeping out of sight amid the overgrowth. He settled in to watch.

It was time to learn everything he could about who came to and went from the office building.

CHAPTER 4
SILVERSHORE CONSULTING

Nighttime in Ravjek was hot. Inexplicably, it got hotter when the sun went down. Shane smoked a cigarette and sipped water from a bottle he'd picked up at the market, sweating and watching the Silvershore office. It was just after midnight, and there was still movement in the building.

Shane had watched eight men leave the office and not return. Each man left in one of the vehicles parked in the lot, heading out at nearly the same time around seven in the evening. He didn't recognize any of them, but he didn't need to. There was no mistaking they were military. They carried themselves like they were expecting trouble, and though none were obviously armed, Shane assumed they all were carrying.

Several vehicles remained in the lot. A guard was stationed on the roof after the sun went down that Shane had almost missed at first but noticed when the man got up to do a quick patrol at dusk. He was armed with a rifle. A second guard was stationed at the parking lot entrance, and a third moved as a shadow beyond the windows inside. It seemed excessive for a consulting firm.

At least eleven men, Shane figured, but he suspected there were also others inside. An office light came on at some point, and though he saw no one in the room, he didn't think the guard patrolling inside had turned it on. Shane had also not seen Luther Washington or Penn Leclerc among those who left or remained.

At just after five in the morning, a black SUV arrived at the office and paused for only a moment with the guard before pulling into a spot. Shane watched a figure in a suit get out of the vehicle under the motion sensor lights and enter a side door. It was not someone he recognized from earlier. Twelve men, then, plus Penn and Luther and the mystery man in the office all night. Fifteen.

As sunrise came, Shane watched the roof guard pack in his weapon. A second figure was with him now. Not another guard, though. Not in the traditional sense, at least. Even at that distance in the dim light of early morning, Shane recognized a ghost when he saw one.

He hadn't seen spirits leave with the others, but that didn't mean they weren't there. The one on the roof was clearly with the guard, and the two even paused to speak for a moment as the guard cleared up his position, packing in not just his weapon but some garbage from a meal he had eaten.

Blakely having a ghost follow him out of the diner, and the roof guard working overnight with one, changed the dynamic of what Shane saw. If everyone at Silvershore had a spirit partner, then he had a team of thirty to deal with.

It was just speculation on Shane's part. He had only seen one ghost, but it was a spirit who had sat through a stakeout. That was not an accident; that was something Carl would do. If not a friend, then absolutely a partner.

Shane fought back exhaustion as the sun rose and the vehicles from the night before returned. They checked in with the gate guard, no more than flashing an ID or even just getting a visual check before heading in. Shane strained to get a closer look at what was happening.

The third vehicle pulled into the lot and while the driver busied himself with something, a second figure emerged. The features were impossible to make out, but the blood was clear. A face covered in a mask of it. A ghost.

Shane swore. Silvershore's mercenaries were paired with spirits across the board. As a unit in the field, it would make them incredibly dangerous and almost impossible to fight. No living force would know what hit them if Silvershore came at them.

It would be difficult to get straight answers from anyone. If they knew Shane could see ghosts, it could dangerously tip the scales against him. That was information they'd want to keep to themselves. It was possible many of their clients didn't even know that was how the unit operated. Their efficiency and skills would seem otherworldly and for good reason, but it would only make Silvershore seem more desirable and more valuable to clients.

A team that could do the impossible. Shane shook his head at the implication.

Blakely's death was still a mystery, but it being either an accident or a consequence of some skirmish with militants was even less likely now. If the unit was doubled up with ghosts, there was no reason for Blakely to have stepped into the line of fire so easily. The ghosts should have been able to eliminate any threat before the living were anywhere near the barrel of a gun.

Shane needed to find Blakely's ghost partner. The half-burned man he'd seen in the diner would be his best source for answers. Finding him could be a challenge, though.

Everyone Shane saw from the night before had returned, and Shane made sure to leave no sign he had been at the ironworks lot before walking back the way he had come.

The trip back to his hotel was a slog in the day's early light, and there were new ghosts on the street who watched him gloomily as he went.

People and spirits clogged the ancient streets, and no one paid the cars driving around them any mind. Shane found himself going with the flow, walking into traffic when it seemed convenient as crosswalks and traffic etiquette were nonexistent.

The man with the round glasses was still at the desk and drinking beer when Shane entered the hotel, though he was wearing a fresh shirt. Neither said anything to the other on Shane's way past the desk.

He returned to his room. The ghost had returned as well, and Shane forced him to leave again. He was tired and not in the mood. The spirit said something in Slovak once more that Shane knew must have been an insult but left through the wall.

The mattress squeaked noisily as Shane lay down and closed his eyes. He was asleep in minutes.

✳ ✳ ✳

"*Žiješ?*"

Shane opened his eyes and stared up at the bloated, purple ghost from the closet. The ghost leaned over his face and poked him in the ribs.

"I don't speak whatever language you're speaking," he said.

The room was darker than it had been when he arrived, the sun having passed to the far side of the building. The faint smell of cooking meat and spices filtered in through the window. The ghost stood up and backed away from him as he sat up.

He had been asleep for the better part of seven hours.

"You need to leave," Shane said to the ghost as he headed to the bathroom.

"*Nemám kam ísť,*" the ghost replied.

Ignoring the spirit, Shane shut the door and took a shower before heading back out. The ghost was still in his room, but he paid him little mind this time, offering him an unamused glance before leaving and locking the door behind him.

He found a taxi a few streets over from the hotel and directed the driver to take him to Silvershore after some issues communicating. The driver spoke little English but was able to follow Shane's directions of where to turn easily enough.

The cab pulled up in front of the glass building, the dark panes reflecting the cab's image at Shane and giving away nothing of what was inside. He glanced up at the cameras fixed on the corners of the building and below the sign bearing the company's name.

When the cab left, Shane looked to his left, making eye contact with the gate guard of the parking lot. The man wore black tactical gear including a vest that looked like Kevlar. He stared blankly at Shane.

A ghost appeared between the two of them, at the edge of the razor-wire fence at the corner of the building, passing into Shane's line of sight. Shane feigned ignorance, keeping his eyes forward for a moment longer as though still staring at the guard, and then turned back to the building and the front door at the end of a cement path ahead of him.

Just as the guard had, the ghost watched with a look of indifference. He was an older man, squarely built, and his torso was riddled with bullet holes. Shane approached the door and reached for the handle, finding it locked. A small intercom to the right crackled as the door shook in his grip.

"Appointment only," a man's voice said over the intercom. Shane looked at it and then pressed the button.

"My name is Shane Ryan. Came here to talk about Davis Blakely."

The intercom crackled and went silent. He stared at the glass door, the tint making it hard to see anything inside.

The ghost by the fence had yet to move, and Shane watched him in his peripheral vision as he waited. Seconds ticked by, and another ghost appeared from inside. The new spirit was nude and almost completely skeletal. He was tall and lithe with off-white flesh that looked like leather pulled across his bones. Hair hung long and wispy from random clumps on his head, while other spots were stark bald.

Shane avoided looking directly at the spirit as it inspected him. The ghost's face was almost a skull, with empty eyes and a missing nose. It had lips like dehydrated bits of meat, stretched above and below long, discolored teeth. His cheeks were like a membrane between cheekbones and jaw, and the cold air poured from him like he was made of ice.

"Anyone there?" Shane asked, pressing the intercom button again.

The radio crackled and went silent once more. The skeletal spirit was close to him now, inspecting him like he was meat on a hook at a market. Even someone unable to see the dead would have felt the ghost's presence and the chill air coming from it.

Shane grunted and rubbed his arm, feeling the pebbled gooseflesh from the cold. A faint hiss came from the ghost's throat, and it receded back into the building. A moment later, the door buzzed, and a heavy lock clicked. He pulled the handle, and the door opened easily in his grasp.

The Silvershore office was like something off Wall Street. The building's location in a gutted, industrial corner of Ravjek gave no sign or expectation of what waited within.

A water fountain trickled gently in the center of a waiting area with leather chairs and a fireplace that lay dormant. The walls were finished in mahogany and silver, and a modern desk in silver and steel with glass accents sat against the closest wall. The man at the desk sat next to a trio of computer monitors. He wore a microphone headset, and while he was not dressed in full tactical gear, he did not try to hide the shoulder harness that held a gun below each arm.

"Mr. Ryan—" the man at the desk began.

"Shane Ryan," another voice corrected before the other man could finish his sentence. Shane's eyes shifted from the armed secretary to a tall man in a suit, one Shane had not seen entering or exiting the building.

The new man's hair was cropped short, and his mouth curled at the left side thanks to a scar through his lip that was made by something large. Behind him, the skeletal ghost stood like a server waiting to take an order at a restaurant.

"Have we met?" Shane asked.

The tall man strode toward him, standing at least six inches above Shane. His suit, held by a single button, buckled when he reached his arm out to shake. Shane couldn't see the gun, but the bulge in the fabric indicated the man wore a shoulder holster as well.

"Lt. Colonel Joseph Copland," he said, offering his hand to Shane. "Retired."

"Shane Ryan," he replied as he shook the offered hand. "As you know."

The ghost watched them both closely, though its eye sockets were empty.

"Davis had told me about you," Copland nodded. "Said he was hoping to get you on board."

"He offered me a job," Shane confirmed. Copland nodded again and turned, putting his arm around Shane and ushering him out of the waiting area.

"Come into my office, and we can talk about that."

"Just kill him," the skeletal ghost whispered. "Let me take his eyes."

Shane said nothing and walked with the man to the next room.

CHAPTER 5
REAPERS

Colonel Copland's office was a testament to some sort of eighties action movie bravado that left Shane at a loss for what to say as he took it all in. A glass display case on the exterior wall was filled with antique weapons ranging from swords to flintlocks and muskets. A second display had more modern firearms, including a pedestal-mounted minigun.

There were taxidermied heads of big-game animals along the walls, everything from lions to rhinos to bears. The largest one, that of a bull elephant with looming tusks, extended several feet above the man's desk. Shane stared at it, wondering how they managed to keep it from falling off the wall.

"Are you a hunter, Ryan?" Copland asked. The door to his office closed automatically behind them, and the skeletal ghost slinked across the room, keeping its empty eyes on Shane the whole time.

"Sometimes," Shane admitted.

"I bagged this one in Tanzania just three years ago. It charged at me from the treeline, and I took it down at no more than four yards away. You never forget a rush like that," Copland said proudly.

"I bet," Shane said. Copland liked to kill, that was very clear.

"So," the colonel said, changing the subject quickly. "Davis Blakely."

"I heard what happened," Shane said.

"Goddamn shame," Copland said, approaching a bar situated under the head of a polar bear. "Drink?"

"No. Thank you," Shane said. Copland poured himself a whiskey with no ice and drank it in one gulp.

"Blakely was a good soldier. Always had his eye on the prize and motivated. He was smart. Too smart for his own good, I guess."

"Meaning?" Shane asked. Copland shrugged.

"You know how it is sometimes. You think you see all the angles, and you lose sight of the idea that you overlooked something. He thought he had the separatists clocked, but he didn't. Took a bullet in the head for it."

"Separatists?" Shane asked.

"Hell, they get a new name every week. Used to be the opposition party. One day they're rebels, the next insurgents, and now, they're separatists. Making trouble for the President, causing strife, killing civilians. They're chaotic and dangerous. Blakely wouldn't recognize that. Wanted to see if they could be handled with diplomacy."

"What happened, then? He was gearing up for a job when we spoke. Seemed to think he was putting together a good team to handle it."

The ghost hissed, and Copland grunted.

"He'd gone in alone to talk to the leader of the group, a would-be leader named Goran. I think they'd been communicating off the books, you know? Nothing officially sanctioned by any client or Silvershore. Blakely wanted to be the hero and bring both sides together. You know how he was. Saved your bacon once, I heard."

Shane said nothing. Blakely had not wanted acknowledgment for saving Shane's life. Hero, yes. But he was not a glory hound.

"Anyway, he went to meet with the man, and the next day, they dragged his body out of some squalid ruins outside of town. I told him Goran wasn't interested in a peaceful meeting, but he wouldn't hear it."

"So he went AWOL on that mission?" Shane asked.

"He's asking too many questions," the ghost said. "Why's he even here?"

"He took matters into his hands, yes," Copland answered Shane. "We're not supposed to operate that way."

"He was alone when he died then," Shane said.

"No way he would have died otherwise. Reaper Company doesn't lose men."

"Reaper Company?" Shane said, raising an eyebrow.

Copland chuckled and shook his head, pouring a second glass for himself.

"Sorry. Officially, we're Silvershore these days, but men don't go in for corporate, sanitized, naming conventions. Reaper Company is the unofficial name."

"Right," Shane said. "I imagine if Davis had someone watching his back, things would have been different."

"Damn right," Copland agreed. "Blakely was the CO here, and our men are loyal, fearless, and without mercy. When we catch Goran, he'll find out why we use the name Reaper."

"So if Davis was CO, who's running the outfit now?"

"He's asking too many questions," the ghost said again. Copland had not acknowledged him at all.

"I took command of the unit after Blakely's death," the retired colonel replied.

It was standard procedure in any military operation, and a lieutenant colonel should have been in command. He outranked Blakely from the get-go. But Silvershore was not supposed to be military. Not officially, anyway. The problem was that Copland was talking very much like they were still active duty and on a mission.

"And this Goran is still in the wind?" Shane asked. Copland nodded.

"He is. For now. But tell me something, Ryan. What brings you to Vakovia? If you're looking to take Blakely up on his offer, I'm afraid that's gone. I'm not looking to fill any spots on my team."

He stared at Shane, his tone making it clear Shane was not wanted or needed.

"Wasn't looking for the job," Shane told him. "I turned Davis down stateside."

"So then… what?"

"He was a friend. When I heard he died so soon after I saw him, I thought I'd come pay my respects."

"Hell of a long way to go for that. His body was shipped home, you know? His grave is in Oregon."

"I know," Shane said. "But I thought I might share a drink with the guys from our old unit as well. Heard Penn Leclerc was with Silvershore. And Luther Washington. Maybe go check out the spot where Davis died."

The ghost growled. Shane continued to ignore him, keeping his eyes on Copland.

"You want to see where Blakely died? Why? You want to get shot, too?"

Shane raised an eyebrow and Copland laughed.

"Come on, soldier. Stop trying to blow smoke up my ass. You're going to visit where he died? Leave a rose and a teddy bear? Respect me enough to tell me the truth. You don't believe the story. You're here on, what, some quest for vengeance? You're going to crack the case and bring Blakely's killers to justice? Something like that?"

"Something like that," Shane replied. Copland's forthrightness was not surprising given the sort of man he appeared to be. He was blunt because he could be. And he didn't fear Shane or anything he thought Shane might learn.

"Blakely was soft, Ryan. You served with him. He was a decent soldier. He was adequate but not exceptional. He ran this outfit because he started it as a civilian. He didn't have the brass to handle the demands of his position. That bit him in the ass and earned him a bullet in his brain. That's what happens when betas try to take on alpha roles. You can feel bad for the man, have a drink for him, but there's no great conspiracy behind it. He got himself killed. End of story."

"Just kill him and be done with it," the ghost added when Copland finished. "He's going to cause more trouble than he's worth."

"I'd still like to see where it happened," Shane said. "Maybe one of your guys can run me out to the spot."

Copland scoffed and shook his head.

"You think my team has time to babysit a civilian? Waste resources taking you on a tour of Ravjek?"

"Then tell me where it happened, and I'll go there myself."

"You want my advice, soldier? Go to the open-air market and get yourself a *lángos*, top it with lots of cheese, and pair it with a nice, cold pilsner. Have a seat, take in the sights, eat your lunch, then pack your shit, get on a plane, and head back home. You don't belong here."

The smile never left the man's face, and Shane simply nodded slowly. Copland had the same tone as a drill sergeant Shane remembered from bootcamp. It was the "don't try me" delivery of a man who didn't allow people to argue with him. Truthfully, nothing would be gained from trying.

Shane would be stunned if Copland hadn't been behind Blakely's death. The man reeked of lies, overconfidence, and malice. But proving it would be harder than going with a gut feeling. And doing anything about it in an office of heavily armed mercenaries and their ghost partners would be harder still.

"Thank you for your time, Colonel," Shane said and turned to leave. Copland laughed.

"That's your one," Copland said as Shane pulled the door open.

"One?" Shane asked, turning to look back. Copland had taken a seat behind his desk and the ghost was holding onto the back of his chair.

"One time you're allowed to turn your back on me. Have a safe flight, Ryan."

Shane grunted and left the office, letting the door click shut behind him. He wondered how Blakely had hooked up with Copland in the first place. Shane couldn't imagine him as a subordinate. Everything must have been an uphill battle dealing with him. Davis had to have known he was a risk. There was something more to their partnership.

A faint murmur of conversation came through the wall as Copland spoke to the ghost. Shane pulled a cigarette from the pack in his pocket and lit it in the lobby.

"You can't smoke in here," the man at the desk informed him.

"Shoot me then," Shane said, inhaling deeply and then blowing the smoke out.

He made his way to the exit and left the building. He had not expected a warm welcome from Silvershore, but he hadn't expected Copland to all but threaten him in his face, either. Copland didn't admit to killing Davis, but his tone and words made it clear that more than the official story was at play.

The fence line ghost had not moved while Shane was inside. It was joined now by Copland's skeletal partner, and they both watched Shane as he headed down the stone path to the street in front of the office.

He glanced at the ironworks factory across the street. The weeds and overgrowth plus the scrap heaps offered suitable cover. He would need to use it again before he was done.

Copland's words were as close to an unspoken threat as Shane had heard. He wasn't sure if the man would even let him leave the country. If he was willing to kill his partner as Shane suspected, his own CO, he would have no qualms about killing Shane.

Shane guessed that Copland knew he wasn't going to leave Vakovia. If that was the case, he would likely put a tail on him. He wouldn't kill him on the road in front of their own offices; it would likely be later in the day. Maybe in the hotel or on a street corner somewhere. Nothing fancy, just a gun to the back of the head when he wasn't expecting it.

Crime in Ravjek was not apocalyptic, but the murder rate shamed a lot of America's more dangerous cities. Police were not known for their efficiency, and many murders in the poorer parts of town went unsolved. Shane's loss would be a blip on the radar. Another American tourist killed in a bad part of town. He'd picked the right hotel for it.

Shane needed more information before he could formulate a proper plan. He needed to find Luther Washington. If he had been gunned down like Blakely, it would have made the news again. But two Silvershore deaths would have been suspicious even to the local police. Just because Shane hadn't seen Luther come to the office didn't mean he was dead.

Either way, Shane would have to track him down.

CHAPTER 6
GROUNDWORK

Luther Washington had gone underground. Shane had not been able to find any sign of the man, and as far as he could discern, their phone call had been the last time anyone had heard from him. Either Silvershore had killed him, or he'd fled in fear they were going to.

Shane found an address for Luther, a little apartment a few miles from his hotel, in one of the Cold War-era buildings where everything looked the same. He took a cab there the next day after he met with Copland.

The building was a concrete monstrosity devoid of charm and noteworthy features. It reminded Shane of an old prison, just without the bars and guards. He knocked on Luther's door and waited maybe two minutes before a burly woman with hair hidden beneath a plaid scarf and a cigarette dangling from her mouth came out of an apartment across the hall.

"He's gone," she said. "Stop your pounding."

Shane had only knocked once, and not that loudly, but he nodded his head anyway.

"Do you know when he left?"

"Two days," she said. "I see him leave in the middle of the night. Pack a bag; didn't even lock the door."

"Did he say anything?"

"I'm not his mother," she replied sourly. "He was noisy. I came to tell him to keep it down. He left. The end."

"Was he alone?"

The woman's eyes narrowed on Shane.

"You're not police. Why you ask so many question?"

"He was a friend. I'm trying to find him."

"Not a good friend if he doesn't tell you where he's going, I think."

"Guess not," Shane agreed.

"You ask the other men. They probably know."

"Which men?"

"Black cars. SUVs. Always together, engines revving in the middle of night, always making noise."

"Were they with him when he left?"

"They come after for him, they wait, they leave. I think maybe you're all criminal." She took the cigarette from between her lips and held it out, using it to point at Shane to accentuate her point.

"No ma'am. Just looking for a friend," Shane said again. The woman scoffed.

"That's what criminal would say."

She retreated to her apartment and slammed the door behind her. Shane returned his attention to Luther's door. Not locked, she'd said.

He turned the knob, and the door fell open. He slipped inside before the woman came out to give him a second round of scolding and closed the door quietly.

The interior of the apartment looked far better than the exterior had led Shane to believe it would. It was no penthouse overlooking Central Park, but it was clean and modern even though the building was very old. The walls were plain and white, and the floor was even finished in hardwood.

Washington had lived sparsely, and there were few decorative accents anywhere. His kitchen was minimal, a stovetop and a refrigerator alongside a Keurig machine. The single-basin sink had a dish-drying rack next to it.

The living area was comprised of two chairs with a throw rug between them, a small coffee table, and a flatscreen TV on the wall. The room was otherwise empty.

The bedroom was more of the same. A bed, a lamp on a nightstand, and a closet. Nothing more. There were several changes of clothes in the closet, but as many hangers hung empty. No shoes or boots that Shane saw.

Shane searched the room from top to bottom and found nothing of interest. On a whim, he took the drawer out of the nightstand and flipped it over. An envelope was taped to the bottom with a thousand American dollars inside.

He grunted and searched the apartment, looking for the obscure spots. He found another thousand behind the toilet tank and another behind the fridge. An envelope behind the TV had already been taken, with only the tape left behind.

It looked to Shane like Luther had taken what he could carry and left in a hurry. A quick search through his drawers showed he had left no paperwork of any importance, not even an old phone bill. The trash cans in the kitchen and the bathroom were empty.

Shane didn't want to rob the man, but accessing his accounts could be risky based on how Copland had received him. If Luther was running with stashed cash, he must have a reason. Shane pocketed the money he'd found and made a mental note to pay Luther back if and when he found him.

He walked to the living room window, hidden behind diaphanous white curtains, and looked outside. The street was busy with foot traffic, cabs, and scooters. A black SUV was parked just a few yards from the building's entrance, and Shane watched it from behind the curtain.

The side-view mirror reflected movement in the driver's seat. Copland had put a tail on Shane. There was no way to know if he was just observing or waiting for a time to do something. At least they were waiting outside and hadn't followed him in.

The temperature of the room dropped noticeably, and Shane stayed still. Luther had no air conditioning, and his concrete building was terrible at temperature regulation. The room was stifling when Shane entered, but now it was tolerable, even bordering on chilly. The ghost partner of his tail had followed him inside.

Shane didn't turn away from the window. He waited there, considering his options. He could play it off like he had with the ghost at Silvershore. Maybe it was only there to observe him. Maybe not, though. He was technically breaking and entering into the apartment of a missing man. It would have been a good opportunity to kill him and make it look like he was committing a crime. It depended on how far Copland was looking to push things. Shane suspected he was looking to push them further.

He turned away from the window. The ghost was standing directly behind him. It had been a young man when he died. His throat had been slashed, and the wash of blood down his uniform still glistened as though it was fresh.

Shane didn't recognize the uniform. Army of some kind but not American, and not recent from the look of it, either. Something European, maybe from the Vietnam War era. The name tag on the uniform read Aguilar.

Their eyes locked, and Shane cursed in his head. He hadn't expected the ghost to be so close, much as it had not expected Shane to be able to see it.

"You see," the ghost said in a thick Spanish accent.

Shane punched the ghost in the mouth as hard as he could, catching him off-guard. Aguilar's head snapped back as he fell to the floor. The idea that Shane would attack was so far from the ghost's mind that he hadn't been ready.

Aguilar cursed in Spanish and spit out a tooth, looking up in time to see Shane dropping on top of him. The ghost yelled, half a growl, as Shane's knees crunched into his pelvis and his fist hit the ghost's face a second time, knocking more teeth loose.

It would not have been Shane's first choice to attack the spirit, but he now knew Shane could see ghosts. Shane didn't want that information getting back to Copland just yet, or his death would be almost assured.

Instead, he took Aguilar by the hair and slammed the ghost's head into the floor several times, keeping the spirit unbalanced and on the defensive. Even if Aguilar had been a soldier in life, he seemed not used to being taken by surprise.

"I'll have your guts," the ghost hissed, pulling at Shane's wrists to force him away.

"No," Shane assured the ghost. "You won't."

As Aguilar pulled Shane's left hand free of his hair, Shane slammed his right hand into the ghost's temple. The spirit's head turned to accommodate the blow and Shane pressed the advantage, pulling his other hand free and twisting the ghost's neck.

Aguilar screamed as Shane's hands squeezed tightly, twisting and crushing at the same time. The resistance of the ghost flesh was not the same as living tissue and bone. It was firm but pliant, and the harder Shane squeezed the more he could feel it giving under the pressure until finally, it gave.

The ghost's head crumbled, first collapsing in like an egg that had shattered and then exploding outward with whatever spiritual force had kept the ghost together.

The blast knocked Shane back as though he'd been tackled, his body absorbing the blow before he landed on the wood floor. His muscles and bones ached like a bruise had sprung to life over every inch of his being. He'd experienced it enough times to know it would fade, but he did not have the luxury of time to wait it out.

The ghost would have been tied to a haunted item, as all spirits were. Everyone in Silvershore-Reaper Company-seemed to have ghost partners, and that meant the living half had to have the haunted item with them to keep their partner nearby.

In the SUV on the street below, whatever item had bound Aguilar to the earthly realm would have just suffered the same fate as the ghost. Haunted items did not endure the destruction of the ghost bound to them.

Shane scrambled to the window and looked out. The door to the SUV was open and the man who had been driving, one of the men he'd observed during his Silvershore recon, was on his knees in the road. He wore black tactical gear from head to toe, but there was blood pooling on the pavement around him, and he was clutching his side. He'd held the haunted item in his pocket then, and when it exploded, it had injured but not killed him.

Shane got to his feet and left the apartment quickly and silently, careful to not disturb the woman across the hall again. Outside the building, a crowd had already gathered around the fallen man. People were yelling in a handful of languages, and Shane could see several on cell phones calling for help.

He worked his way into the crowd, just another onlooker, and got close enough to see the soldier. He was slumped against the side of the SUV, blood still coming from a wound somewhere on his side or back. The explosion might have taken out his liver, judging from the location of the blood. Bad luck for his choice of pockets. The man was dead by the time he got close enough to observe him.

A siren was wailing in the distance, meaning an ambulance and the police would arrive soon. If Copland was monitoring the local police band, they would probably be on the way soon as well. It seemed unlikely that the fallen soldier had time to call for help, but it was possible. Shane needed to be elsewhere before anyone showed up.

Shane slipped from the crowd and walked at a casual pace away from the body and off the street, heading down a random side road. He was just another pedestrian out for a walk and would remain so for a few blocks to not rouse suspicion.

With any luck, Copland and the others would be confused by what happened. No witnesses would place Shane at the scene when the man died, and Aguilar couldn't share his insights. Even if they suspected Shane, they wouldn't be able to explain what happened. Not for a while, anyway.

Shane was blocks away when he ducked into a small cafe and ordered coffee before sitting by a window to watch the street. He sipped his coffee and pondered his options going forward. With Luther off the grid and Reaper Company potentially on his trail and out for blood, his only options were to leave the country or flip the script.

Leaving the country was not a real option. Copland would have someone posted at the airport and train stations. Shane would have to take the fight to Copland.

He finished his coffee and had a cigarette.

"Do you have a pen and some paper?" he asked the barista in the cafe. The woman looked perplexed but handed him a notepad when he pointed to it. He filled a sheet of paper quickly and then gave the pad back to the woman with his thanks before leaving.

He had work to do.

CHAPTER 7
HUNTER

When Shane returned to his hotel, the lobby ghost was staring at the wall and Milos was drinking another beer. It would take Copland a while to track Shane here since there were no records and his tail was gone. Hopefully, he had enough time.

"Milos," Shane said, approaching the desk. The man blinked behind his tiny glasses.

"No refund," he said. Shane shook his head.

"No. You said you could get me things if I needed them."

"You want girl? Blonde?" Milos asked.

Shane put an envelope of cash he'd taken from Luther's apartment on the counter along with the hastily scrawled note he'd written at the cafe.

"Can you get these things?" he asked.

Milos picked up the list and read it. His eyes drifted from the list to Shane and back, then he took the envelope and counted the cash.

"No refund," he repeated.

"How long?"

"Come back two hours. Maybe three."

Shane raised his eyebrows.

"Everything? Just three hours?"

"Everything. Probably Russian. Good for you?"

"Good," Shane agreed. The turnaround seemed fast, but Vakovia was proving to be an interesting and volatile place. He'd be happy if Milos could come through with just a portion of it. He was overpaying for quick service if nothing else.

Shane headed to his room to wait and stay out of sight until things were ready. He needed to get to Copland as soon as he could, but the Silvershore office was out of the question. Shane had to get him alone somewhere and find out the truth about what happened. If Copland hadn't pulled the trigger, he knew who did. Shane would get the real story.

Time dragged on while he waited and smoked, watching the street out of his window for any sign of Silvershore men. Not a single car that had been built in the past twenty years drove down the street.

It was early evening when Shane left the room again, his ghost roommate questioning him in Slovak once more. Milos looked like he hadn't moved at all in the interim, but a pair of boxes sat on the desk next to him.

"Your supplies," the man said. Shane looked through them quickly. It was most of what he'd requested. Maybe not the quality he hoped for, but it would do.

"Keys," Milos added, pushing a keychain toward him.

Shane took the keys, stacked the boxes, and headed out the door to the street where a half-rusted-out Volkswagen waited. He opened the back door with the key and dropped the boxes inside before getting behind the wheel.

Ugly as it might have been, the car looked like every third vehicle on the street, and it ran. Shane drove from the hotel, taking a circuitous route from the neighborhood and around the city toward Silvershore.

The sun was just setting when Shane arrived. He parked near the building, in the parking lot of a textile plant that was still in operation.

Shane pulled a pair of binoculars from one of the boxes Milos had given him and adjusted the lenses. He watched Silvershore, focusing on the gate. A guard and a ghost were stationed there, and everything looked to be business as usual. The roof guard had also taken up his position for the night.

A handful of vehicles came and went over the next hour. Once the sun set, Shane watched through the green glow of night vision. It was another two hours before he saw Copland leaving the building.

There was no sign of the skeletal ghost, but Shane knew he had to be nearby. Even if he didn't get in the SUV, as long as Copland had the spirit's haunted item, he'd be forced to join the colonel wherever he went.

Shane watched the vehicle pull out of the lot and turn toward the textile factory. He waited until the SUV drove past and then started his car, keeping the lights off before creeping onto the road and following the man.

He kept Copland at a suitable distance, tracking him as closely as he dared. The SUV stuck out like a sore thumb on the streets of Ravjek, making it easy to follow even from a distance. He didn't need to get made before he discovered where the colonel was going.

Shane hoped to track the man to his home, but the SUV followed a straightforward path toward the city's downtown and the glass skyscrapers that dominated the landscape.

The streets filled with more cars, and Shane had to close the gap between himself and Copland to keep the vehicle in sight. Newer and fancier vehicles shared the road now, and Shane found himself alongside a Lamborghini, four cars behind the SUV at a red light.

The lights of downtown Ravjek were a mix of blinding LEDs and gaudy neon speckled between modern businesses and relics of the ancient world they'd replaced. There were restaurants with valet parking alongside noisy nightclubs and what looked like an art gallery opening. The rich of Vakovia claimed the downtown at night while the poor stayed elsewhere.

The Volkswagen, which Shane asked to be inconspicuous, was starting to look more and more out of place. He switched lanes, keeping Copland in sight, and hedged his bets on how long it would take the man to leave the area and head someplace less crowded. It didn't happen.

The SUV pulled over in front of a building lit by black lights that cast the entrance in a vivid purple glow. Shane drove past and pulled over a block ahead, watching Copland get out and hand his keys to a valet before heading through the black-lit door.

A European nightclub, Shane thought. *Perfect place for a deranged retired colonel in his fifties.*

He rifled through the boxes Milos had given him and pulled out the gear he'd requested. He changed out of his clothes and into the tactical gear he'd been given. Black combat pants that were a bit snugger than he would have liked, a plain T-shirt, and a vest over the top. Milos had even found a genuine Marine Kabar for him and a pair of iron knuckles that he slipped into his pockets along with a bundle of black zip ties. His iron rings would be fine for taking care of ghosts, but he expected his fists would meet more than dead flesh soon enough.

Shane got out of his car and headed back down the street toward the club entrance. There was a lineup at the door as well-dressed men and women waited for a man with massive shoulders and sunglasses to let them get into the building. Copland, it seemed, had a standing invitation and was already inside.

The people in line were all younger than Shane, better dressed, and clearly wealthier. Heavy bass music boomed from inside, and the people outside were either talking loudly on their phones or yelling at each other.

Shane passed the line and the doorman and just walked to the entrance. He made it inside but was quickly stopped by the huge man at a dark hallway.

"*Iba pozvanie,*" the man said in a deep, angry voice.

"Come again?" Shane said, raising his voice to be heard over the music in the club. The big man held up a clipboard of names.

"Invite only!" he shouted.

"Oh," Shane said, cocking his head to look at the list on the board although it was too dark to see. He lifted his hand, about to point out a name, and punched the guard in the throat.

The big man choked and crumpled to his knees, gurgling, and holding his throat. Seeing nobody had seen what just happened, he punched the guard once more. The man slumped and Shane grunted as he pulled the unconscious man away from the door.

"They should buy me some time before they discover you." He patted the man on the shoulder.

Shane entered the club.

✳ ✳ ✳

The bass of the music was so intense that it shook Shane's bones. The black-light motif continued inside. Everything white glowed like it was electric, even people's teeth. The center of the building was a massive open dance floor. Several hundred people writhed and bounced to the music, their bodies twisting and bumping against one another.

A DJ at the far end of the room glowed like the sun in white, swaying with the beat. To his left was a bar with bottles of expensive alcohol. Above him, a wall of windows showed some kind of office or suite on the other side. Men in suits drifted around, holding drinks, and ignoring the club below.

That Copland had business in such a place was almost as baffling to Shane as Blakely's death. Nothing about the club screamed "big-game hunting mercenary".

Shane scanned the crowd from the entrance, trying to see above people's flailing hands and through flashing lights and bursts of smoke from a machine. Faces appeared and vanished as dancers spun and twisted in and out of sight.

He caught a glimpse of a man in a suit at the bar but couldn't tell for sure if it was Copland. Too many people in the way made it impossible to tell. He pushed his way into the throng. The humid air, the heat of the day, the closeness, and the dancing made the club cloying and unpleasant. All the perfume and body spray worn by the patrons did little to mask the underlying smell of sweat and flesh.

Shane weaved through the crowds, using his body to deflect the more vigorous dancers and sometimes his hands to position people out of his way. He reached the bar, an all-glass structure lit with searing blue lights. A bartender yelled at him, words lost to the deafening beat, and he just shook his head. If the man he'd seen was Copland, he was gone now. Shane couldn't imagine he was out on the dance floor.

He lifted his head and looked up. The men on the second floor were still milling about and talking. Shane didn't recognize any of them, but they had something in common. Like Copland, none of them looked like men who belonged in a European dance club. They were older businessmen, well-dressed but leaning toward tacky and wearing what looked like expensive watches and jewelry. That was where he'd find the colonel.

Shane moved from the bar to the DJ stand. Beyond the DJ was another security guard, and behind him was a door. The label was not English, but Shane guessed it was letting patrons know it was private. That was what he needed.

He skirted the DJ stand and headed toward the security guard.

"I'm heading up," he said, otherwise ignoring the guard in hopes that confidence might work a second time. It did not.

"Name?" the man asked. He also had a clipboard.

Shane debated whether punching this man in the throat was the best course of action, but something caught his attention before he could decide one way or the other. A figure moved through the crowd toward him. causing others to move out of the way. But it was clear that they were not doing so consciously. They were avoiding the cold.

The ghost was a woman with hair pulled back into a thick, tight braid. She was muscular like an athlete, and vast swaths of flesh were missing from many areas where her skin was exposed.

She moved with a purpose toward Shane and whether Copland knew he could see ghosts yet didn't matter. This one was coming straight for him.

She swept in quickly, with the cold coming off her a relief against the stifling heat of the club. Shane slipped a hand into his pocket, four fingers lacing through the iron knuckles as he closed his fist and pulled his hand free.

The ghost was on him, and he hit her with a right cross. Iron met ghost flesh, and she vanished, shot back to wherever her haunted item was kept.

To the guard, it looked like Shane had thrown a punch at thin air. But he saw Shane was armed, and that was enough.

Shane felt a hand on his shoulder as the guard tried to take him into custody. He shot his arm back, elbowing the guard in the nose, and then turned on him quickly, laying him out with a single punch from the iron knuckles. The man went down like a sack of potatoes, Shane catching him halfway through his collapse and easing him to the floor as best he could.

"Sorry, big fella," Shane muttered.

By the time he stood, the ghost was back. She landed a quick jab into Shane's gut, and he stumbled back. The vest had taken the bulk of the hit, but it was still powerful enough to make him gasp.

"Ready to die, American?" the ghost asked, her voice gravelly and deep.

"Not really," Shane answered simply.

CHAPTER 8
EXPOSED

The ghost was trained to fight. If she'd had a weapon, she would have been even deadlier, but she was skilled enough at hand-to-hand combat that Shane was on defense as much as offense.

They traded blows as the bass of the music shook the room and strobe lights blasted them in the face with bursts of white and blue and red. Dancers could only see Shane, his hands balled into fists, swinging his arms, and occasionally kicking out. They continued their ritual, undeterred and unaware that he fought for his life in their midst.

He had been backed onto the dance floor and bounced from body to body like a pinball, avoiding the living while he lashed out at the ghost. Twice, he had clipped her with the iron knuckles, but each time she was back in moments, indicating her haunted item was within just a few yards of their fight at most.

When she returned the third time, her strategy changed. Lights flashed, the floor shook, and the ghost stayed out of Shane's reach. He stalked her through the crowd as she ducked from dancer to dancer, hiding behind the living and grinning at Shane.

The beat changed, and the ghost stopped. She took hold of a man decked out in heavy silver chains and threw him at Shane, lifting him from the ground and tossing him like a bag of trash.

The man cried out in surprise and then pain as Shane ducked aside, letting the man hit others and fall to the ground. The crowd surged, some shocked and concerned, but most of them were totally unaware of what happened.

She grabbed a second dancer and Shane went in for a quick attack, punching the ghost's hand and forcing her back again. If he let her, she'd continue to use the living as shield and weapons if she didn't kill some of them outright.

As soon as the ghost vanished, he left the dance floor, heading toward the door at the rear of the club. He reached it just as she appeared again.

"Leaving so soon?" she said as he opened the door.

"Private party," he explained, ducking through the door, and forcing her to follow.

They were in a stairwell, the music heavily muffled save for the bass. The ghost's smile was hateful, and her pale blue eyes were fixed on Shane like a predator stalking prey.

"Who taught you that trick?" she asked, nodding to the knuckles on his hand. Shane shook his head.

"A man can't give away all his secrets, can he?"

She shrugged.

"Take them to your grave, then," she said, lunging for a low attack.

She had moved to take out Shane's legs. Doing so exposed the back of her head and Shane caught her ponytail braid, pulling her harshly against the staircase and then dragging her as he backed away from her attack.

"You working for Copland?" he asked, forcing her face-down and kneeling between her shoulder blades.

"I'm going to pull out your spine," the ghost replied, trying to push herself up. Shane slipped the knuckles back into a pocket and reached down, grabbing the ghost's right middle finger, and snapping it back. She screamed, and he grabbed the next finger.

"Who sent you after me?" he asked.

"Who taught you this? How are you able to—"

Shane broke her index finger.

"Who sent you?" he asked again.

"Everyone saw your picture. Everyone knows your face, American.

Shane Ryan of the American Marines. It's not just me."

"They put a hit on me?" he said. Copland worked faster than Shane had guessed.

"I can make it quick. Others won't," the ghost told him, writhing again.

"Who's upstairs? What are they here for?"

"Why do you care? You're a dead man."

"I'd be more concerned with my own well-being if I were you," Shane pointed out. The ghost laughed at him, genuinely amused.

"I'm already dead, fool. What can you do to me?"

She struggled beneath him again, and he leaned forward, pinning her head down. He was wasting time and losing track of Copland.

"Last chance," he told her, his forearm pressed against her head to hold her in place.

"When I rip out your guts—"

The crunch of her neck cut off the end of her sentence. Shane had twisted it backward. She faced him now, a stunned look on her face as her eyes twitched. He applied pressure and finished the job, causing the ghost's head to burst.

The blast of energy was all but silenced by the overwhelming beat of the music outside. He got to his feet and took a moment to steady himself before heading up the stairs to the second floor.

The bass thrum resonated through the stairs. Shane stood outside a wooden door with gold accents. He slipped the iron knuckles back over the fingers of his right hand and tried the knob. It turned easily in his hand.

The room beyond looked like some sort of VIP box seat for a sporting event. There were couches, a bar, tables set up with fancy hors d'oeuvres, and bits of trash scattered across the floor. A mangled piece of metal sat on a center table, burn marks darkening the table's wooden finish.

Likely the ghost's haunted item, Shane thought.

Everyone was gone except for a security guard standing at a pair of double doors at the far wall.

"Hands," the man said in a British accent.

The guard was not like the club security. This one was dressed nearly the same as Shane. He wore full tactical gear and had a Beretta M12 trained on Shane the moment he entered the room.

Shane raised his hands and sighed.

"Late to the party, huh?" he said.

"You don't know how late, mate," the soldier said, approaching carefully without lowering his weapon.

"Reaper Company?" Shane asked. The man didn't look familiar, but he fit the profile. The soldier smiled grimly.

"What happened to Mathilda?" he countered, reaching for the metal on the table, gun still trained at his target.

"Angry lady from the club? Think she's dancing," Shane answered.

The soldier reached Shane and took up position behind him with his gun to the back of Shane's head.

"Try again," the man said. He tossed the chunk of metal to the floor in front of Shane before doing a quick pat down, hitting Shane's pockets and pulling out the knife.

"Never got her name. Mathilda, was it?"

The gun dug into the back of his skull.

"Tell me what happened, or I will put you down just like Blakely," the soldier warned.

"You're going to do that anyway," Shane replied.

"Where is she?" the man yelled, kicking out Shane's legs from behind, who fell on his knees. The soldier was on him in an instant, the barrel of his weapon pressed to the top of Shane's skull. "Last chance."

"Funny," Shane grunted, tightly squeezing the iron knuckles that the soldier had overlooked in his fist. "I said the same thing to your girl before I popped her head like a melon."

The soldier grabbed Shane's collar and pulled him around so the two were facing each other. Shane swung low and drove the iron knuckles into the man's groin as hard as he could.

The man's body spasmed as he collapsed. The gun fell from his hand, but Shane ignored it, ramming his shoulder into the man's gut and knocking him back to the ground.

Shane was on top of him in an instant. He planted his knee in the soldier's groin and removed a zip tie from his pocket, securing the man's wrists through his own belt buckle.

"What was Copland doing here?"

The other man's face was still a mask of agony. Shane shifted his knee and the man screamed, the sound lost in the music. Based on the soldier's reaction, he had done some permanent damage. He was still alive, though.

"Copland," Shane asked again. "If you can't talk, then I have no use for you."

"You think I care what you do to me?" the soldier sputtered.

"Seems like it," Shane said, grinding his knee down harder and causing the man to scream again.

It took the soldier a long moment to compose himself, breathing heavily while sweat beaded on his face, and tears at the corners of his eyes.

"I'm as dead as you are," he choked out. "Might as well do it yourself."

"Tell me what Copland was doing here. Where he's going. Give me something, and you can still walk away."

The man laughed mirthlessly and haltingly, gasping for breath between.

"You're dumber than you look," the soldier muttered.

Annoyed and certain he was not going to make progress, Shane pushed the man's head to the side and forced his forearm across the side of his neck. The soldier sputtered and struggled but only briefly as the pressure on his arteries cut off the blood supply to his brain. He was unconscious in seconds, and Shane left alive.

Let them think he'd given up information in exchange for his life.

Outside of the double doors was a hallway that led to another stairwell and a rear exit to the building. Copland and the other men in suits were long gone. Shane's ability to destroy ghosts had been exposed and he had nothing to show for it.

The men at the VIP lounge looked wealthy and connected. Copland had to have been meeting with a client, or a prospective one. Someone with money to spend on a team of highly trained mercenaries. Maybe someone behind Blakely's death.

The questions and lack of answers were not doing Shane any favors. He left through the rear exit and circled back to his car, looking for any sign that Copland or the Reapers might be tailing him. If anyone else had been sent to watch him, they were keeping well out of sight.

The ghost had told Shane she'd seen his picture. Copland had put his name out there, probably after what happened at Luther's apartment. It could have gone beyond the company, but Shane believed this was the kind of thing Copland would want to keep in-house. They were going to clean up their mess, and that meant more than a dozen mercenaries and ghosts with his name and face burned into their brains for the foreseeable future.

Shane returned to the hotel, taking a meandering route and keeping his eyes on his rearview as he went, searching for any sign of a tail. The hotel was suitable cover but wouldn't remain that way. He had little faith in Milos' loyalty. It would be compromised soon enough.

Including the cabbie who had dropped him there and a handful of ghosts who had seen him come and go, there were witnesses who could identify Shane. His appearance wasn't so easily forgotten that he could vanish in a crowd. It was time to move on.

He parked the car a block from the hotel and kept to the shadows as best he could on his return to the unmarked building. It was nearly midnight, and the place did not merit streetlights. The neighborhood was as silent as ever, meaning sounds of the city drifted in from blocks away but little was happening in the immediate area.

The lobby ghost was missing when Shane entered. Milos was asleep at his desk, his open beer on the desktop barely touched.

Shane crept up the stairs and made his way down the hall to his room. The floorboards squeaked underfoot as he walked, making him wince with each sound. In the hotel's silence, every creak sounded like a blaring alarm.

He reached the door and pulled out his key, pausing when he felt the looseness of the doorknob in his hand. He turned it slowly and quietly. It was unlocked.

He felt a chill set into his bones despite the heat, and his pulse quickened. Shane opened the door and peered into the room. The lights were out, and the dark room appeared empty from the door.

"*Niekto je tu,*" a voice whispered from behind him. His ghost roommate was in the hall, looking into the room over Shane's shoulder.

"*Nevstupovat,*" the ghost added.

Shane was not alone. Someone was waiting in the dark.

CHAPTER 9

RUN FOR YOUR LIFE

Shane had left his passport and some money in the room, taped under the bedside table drawer. He didn't want to risk taking it with him, and it had been his only option at the time. In hindsight, that was a bad idea.

He dug into his pocket for his iron knuckles and took a step into the dark room. The floor creaked underfoot, the same spot he thought would make a good early warning if anyone snuck up on him in his sleep.

There was no time to even curse. A shadow rushed from the darkness toward Shane, tackling him in the doorway and out into the hall. The freezing hands of a ghost clawed at him as it took hold of his neck.

In the dimly lit hall, Shane could just make out the scarred face of a ghost he'd seen during his Silvershore recon. Someone had removed his ears before death, and his mouth had been sliced into a much wider smile. The eyes were focused and clear, looking into Shane's with a hateful glare.

"Colonel Copland sends his regards," the ghost hissed, a wicked smile spreading across his sliced mouth.

Cold hands clamped over Shane's throat and the tips of the ghost's fingers dug into his flesh. He began squeezing, choking Shane even as his fingernails drew blood.

Shane punched the ghost in the chin. There was a quick popping sound as the ghost's jaw broke and twisted left, but it vanished in the same instant, the iron forcing it back to wherever it had come from.

"*Nebol sám,*" Shane's roommate said, his tone excited as he pointed back to the room.

Shane sat up in time to see a second ghost descending upon him. This one was slighter of frame but in far worse condition than the first. The ghost's hands had been stripped of flesh and muscle nearly up to the elbow, and the bones were burned nearly black. What flesh remained on the spirit was just as burned. It looked like he'd died holding an explosive, and his spirit was stuck perpetually in the initial moments of incineration.

The spirit garbled some words from a burned mouth and swiped at Shane with a skeletal hand. He rolled aside to avoid the attack. The ghost kept after him, and Shane scrambled back to the stairs until his back hit the railing.

An arm slipped around his neck from behind, and Shane realized the first ghost had returned. He held Shane tightly in place but was not putting on enough pressure to choke him. He was holding him for the burned ghost to attack.

With an unintelligible growl, the burned spirit came at Shane with blackened claws. Shane caught his arm and used the ghost's momentum to pull him off-balance as he raised his legs. The burned arm came down over Shane's knee and broke. The bone splintered, and the ghost wailed as Shane pulled the hand away and tossed it aside, leaving the ghost with half a forearm.

He punched the arm holding him, banishing the spirit once more as iron hit ghostly flesh, and then pushed off the railing toward the ghost still reeling from the loss of its arm.

The burned ghost growled and formed words Shane couldn't understand. He was expecting it to make another attack, but it backed off instead, the malice clear in its eyes.

Shane was tense and ready. He watched the ghost and waited for the arrival of his partner. The dim hallway lights flickered. The ghost smiled, a gesture both mad and ominous, and then he lifted his one good hand and snapped the charred, skeletal fingers. The lights went out.

The darkness that overtook the hallway was unnatural. No light from below crept up the stairs, and nothing from around the cracks in doors filled the space. It was all-consuming as though a bag had been pulled over his head.

Shane pushed his back against the nearest wall, feeling the texture of the ancient wallpaper scraping against the back of his vest as he moved slowly. He dropped a hand into his pocket and felt the cool metal of his lighter.

The top of the lighter moved under his thumb. The hinge of the lid clicked, and the wheel scraped as the flint sparked. The small flame burst to life, and Shane held the lighter up. The hallway was gone.

He was nowhere. The walls and doors had vanished. Even the floor was an impenetrable darkness at his feet. The light he had created illuminated himself and nothing else, a small sphere of flickering flame in which Shane was the only thing that existed.

He grunted and looked around at the emptiness. It was not the most unique trick a ghost had pulled off, but it would serve its purpose of being disorienting.

Shane still felt the wall behind him. The ghostly illusion wasn't powerful enough to take it away and make him think he was lost in nothing.

He paced down the length of the wall until he found a door. His fingertips brushed against the wood, and he looked directly across from it at the empty space of the void that surrounded him. In reality, the door to his room was right there. The ghost's illusion obscured it, but if the door behind him was still real, then so was his door across from it.

Nothing moved. The second ghost should have returned, and if he had, he was playing possum like his handless friend. But that made no sense. Why not go in for the kill?

He stared into the darkness where his room should have been and took a step forward. An icy wind rushed past, and the flame of the lighter flickered and almost went out.

Maybe they had never intended to kill him. Maybe the ghosts were just there to keep him busy.

Shane rushed into the darkness. The floor squealed underfoot, and he was in his room again. The illusion faltered as he reached out, found the door, and slammed it shut. His room returned, but the scarred ghost returned as well.

The spirit pinned Shane to the newly closed door, smiling his deformed smile in Shane's face before gnashing what teeth remained in his mouth.

"You're more trouble than you're worth," the ghost said.

Shane responded by smashing his forehead into the ghost's nose. The cold flesh bent and crunched, and the ghost let go, screaming in rage as he stumbled back, holding his broken face.

With the second spirit still in hiding, Shane did not have time to play. He took the ghost by the back of the head and forced it down as he raised his knee to meet it. The ghost's face crunched again as more of his skull cracked.

A second knee to the face changed the tone of the ghost's pained wails. He pulled and jerked like an animal trying to escape from a trap, but Shane did not let go.

"Sorry, what did you say?" Shane asked, slamming his knee into the ghost's face a third time. "I couldn't hear over your shrieking."

The ghost's skull crunched loudly. Shane pulled the spirit up by the back of his neck and pressed him face-first against the wall before grasping his head in both hands. There was only the briefest moment of struggle before his already-ruined skull gave under the pressure of Shane's hands.

Shane was launched back against the far wall as the ghost exploded. The narrow space made the burst of energy hit harder, and he was tossed back hard enough to knock the wind from his lungs.

He crumpled to the floor, gasping, and sucking at the air, trying to fill his chest. The lights in the room flickered, and the air grew colder. A hand like ice closed around Shane's neck and lifted his head. The burned ghost glared down at him and held up his splintered arm, pointing the shattered tip at Shane's face.

The ghost growled out garbled words, the broken arm poised to strike as Shane struggled to breathe.

From the outer hallway, another figure appeared. It moved swiftly and tackled the one-handed ghost before it could follow through on its threat. The skeletal hand pulled free of Shane's neck as the ghost was knocked away from him.

Shane gasped, drawing in air as quickly as he could, and watched as a third ghost he had never seen fought with the burned spirit. The two rolled and struggled, making it hard for Shane to focus on what he was seeing or who had even come to his aid.

The new ghost was thin and smaller than the burned spirit. They wrestled for position until Shane could see it was the ghost of a woman barely out of her teens. Her head was shaved nearly bald, and there were no eyes in her face, only dark, half-scabbed wounds where they had been cut free.

The burned ghost stabbed the newcomer in the gut with his shattered arm, using the bone like a spear to skewer her abdomen. Unable to feel pain, she barely reacted, opting instead to drive an elbow into her attacker's neck before leaning in and biting off one of his ears.

A garbled scream erupted from the burned ghost's throat, and he reeled back, still on the floor, aiming his shattered hand for a second strike, this time at the girl's face. Shane caught the ghost's elbow before he could follow through and pulled back. He brought his boot down hard on the ghost's shoulder as he twisted the arm, popping it out of its joint, and tearing it from the ghost's body.

The eyeless ghost gazed up at Shane with the ruined pits of her eye sockets and scowled.

"Don't need help, chief," she hissed.

To prove her point, she wrapped her arms and legs around the still-stunned ghost and pulled his head to the side and then finally away from his body.

The release of energy was less intense, and the girl took the brunt of it while Shane was merely buffeted by it. She stayed on the floor on all fours for a moment after their opponent had been destroyed before getting to her feet.

She did not come for Shane, and though her eyes were gone, he got the impression she was sizing him up. The ghost was much shorter than he was, barely five feet tall, and she probably would have been a hundred pounds in life if she was lucky. She wore an oversized Army surplus jacket, combat boots, and tights, as well as a ratty band T-shirt that now had a hole in it from the other ghost's arm.

"Ease up, Kat," a new voice said. Shane recognized it immediately, even before Luther Washington stepped into the room.

He was bulkier than Shane remembered. He'd put on muscle since their time serving together, but his face was still young. He had dark hair, a dark complexion, and clear brown eyes that made him look a little too innocent for his line of work.

Luther was dressed like he was out for a walk, a pair of plain khakis and a light jacket over a polo shirt. A gun was holstered beneath the jacket, but nothing else made him look like he was a Marine on the run from a group of mercenaries.

"You need to leave the city, sir," Luther said.

"I told you to stop calling me sir," Shane pointed out. He turned his attention to the ghost that was still focused on him. "She with you?"

"Kat's my partner, yeah. Copland likes to call them 'spectral assets'. He's got a million terms for a million things. I prefer 'partner'."

"Kat. Alright," Shane said. "You're tougher than you look, by the way."

"Damn right I am," the ghost agreed. He smiled at her and walked to the window of his hotel room.

"They'll be here soon," Luther said, knowing what Shane was looking for. Someone had to have brought the two ghosts here. They were close.

Shane got a good look at the room for the first time now. It had been thoroughly tossed. His money and passport were gone. They'd even taken his clothes. Copland didn't want him to leave town. Not that Shane planned to go just yet.

"Ryan, are you hearing me? They made you a target. You need to go."

"I know I'm a target," Shane answered. "But so are they."

CHAPTER 10
BLACK OPS

There was nothing left to gather from his room. In the lobby, Shane paused to warn Milos that he might want to make himself scarce. The man was in the same position he had been when Shane went upstairs, with his beer still full. He reached across the desk and touched the man's arm. He was cold.

Shane grunted. He barely knew Milos, and he seemed as sketchy as anyone Shane had met, but they hadn't needed to kill him. Copland wasn't a soldier who killed because it was the job he'd been assigned, though. He killed because he liked to do it. He liked the hunt, and he enjoyed taking his prize. The only difference between his trophy hunting and what he was doing now was that he was using other soldiers, his company, as a weapon.

"Dead?" Luther asked.

Shane nodded, and they left the lobby and headed for the street. Kat followed close behind as Shane led them away from the building, obscured in the shadows of nearby buildings until they reached the corner.

The Volkswagen waited where Shane had left it. He paused then hid in the shadows of some unlabeled building. Back the way they had come, two figures appeared on the street, armed and dressed all in black. They headed into the hotel.

"Genereaux and Potts," Luther said quietly. "We just took out their partners."

When the soldiers were out of sight, Shane led the others toward his car and got behind the wheel.

"This is what you're driving?" Kat asked. Her accent wasn't

European. If anything, she sounded like she might have come from California.

"Inconspicuous," Shane explained.

"Piece of crap," the ghost countered. "Luther, we gotta ditch this guy and go while he's keeping the company distracted."

"Kat," Luther said firmly. She sighed and slumped against the back seat.

"Sorry for wanting to keep you alive, man. Just my job and everything."

Shane started the engine and headed up the street, unsure of where he was going but needing distance between them and the hotel.

"So, you guys have been running ops with ghosts? How long has that been a thing?"

"How long have you been able to see them?" Luther countered.

"Hey, not just that. He killed Miggs, man. With his bare hands," Kat added.

Luther stared at Shane unsurely.

"You can fight them?"

"Killed him, man! Crushed his head. Nearly killed himself, but still, I saw it," Kat said.

"Not killed," Shane pointed out. "You're already dead. Just destroyed. Now, can you answer my question?"

"Blakely recruited me a couple of years ago. I got shot north of Kabul, just missed my heart. Was in surgery for a while and died on the table twice. Came to, and there's a guy with half his skull missing the next bed over. First ghost I ever saw. Been seeing them ever since. I don't know how Blakely found out; I only told the base shrink, and those files are supposed to be confidential."

"A lot of things are supposed to be one way but they're another," Shane replied.

"I guess so," Luther conceded. "Blakely comes at me with an offer, has his own ghost with him, and I accepted. It seemed like good money and a good job. You knew Blakely, sir. He was a good guy."

"He was," Shane agreed. "So, when did things go south?"

"Copland," Luther said without hesitation. "Someone was backing Silvershore. Blakely wasn't rich; he was a grunt like the rest of us. He didn't have business contacts, but whoever backed Silvershore did. They wanted Copland on board. He was supposed to be oversight, a more polished and experienced voice to temper Blakely's, I guess."

"So, whoever backed Silvershore knew Blakely's secret? That you guys used ghosts? They needed him to recruit others who could do the same?"

"Maybe," Luther said. "I wasn't in the loop on that sort of thing. But it's an entire company of guys who can see the dead, so it's not hard to figure out that part."

"And her?" Shane asked, looking in the mirror.

"Kat? We got paired up at the start."

"That's right," Kat confirmed.

"How'd you get recruited?"

Kat laughed, still slumped in the backseat, playing with the zip on her jacket.

"You ever been dead, man? It's boring as hell. I was stuck behind a warehouse in San Diego since nineteen eighty-eight. I made a deal to get out, see the world, have some fun, and all I gotta do is keep this fool from getting shot."

"What about now?" Shane asked.

"What do you mean what about now?" she replied suspiciously.

"Luther turned on the group, right? That makes him a target now. And you're still… partners? You're not working for Copland still, are you?"

"Man," Kat said, her voice rising to a whine as she looked at Luther. "Can we ditch this chump yet? Questioning my integrity in your crap-ass car? No—"

"She's good," Luther interrupted. "She doesn't work for Copland. Hates the guy's guts."

"He kills animals," Kat complained. "Only jerks do that."

"Right," Shane said. "So, what the hell happened? Why is Blakely dead?"

"I don't know," Luther answered simply.

Shane pulled a cigarette from a pocket in his vest and lit it. He was weaving down streets he hadn't traveled before and was not sure where they were. They were just putting distance between themselves and Copland's men.

"You don't know anything?"

"Silvershore might not be a sanctioned military outfit, but they run ops the same way. I get orders, I follow orders. No one explains to me what the brass is doing. I get mission briefs when I'm about to do a mission. That's all, sir."

"You don't hear things?" Shane asked Kat. She scowled at him.

"Everyone in the company has a spectral asset. If Kat went sneaking around, she'd get caught. We don't operate like that. There's supposed to be trust there," Luther explained.

Shane grunted and shook his head.

"So what made you run?"

"Blakely died, and Copland assumed command. I already had an issue with the man. I don't like the way he does things, and I never have. The entire rest of the crew was recruited by him. Only me and Leclerc were Blakely's picks, and when Leclerc showed up dead, it was easy enough to see the writing on the wall."

"Leclerc is dead?" Shane said. He had heard nothing about that, though it was no surprise that Copland hadn't mentioned it.

"Found him the morning you first called me. Two through the back of the head in his shower. That's why I cut and run."

"They're cleaning up Blakely's loose ends then Copland assumes full control, huh? How did you get away?"

"I knew someone was coming to kill me," Luther answered. "With Blakely and Leclerc down, I was the odd man out. There was always some tension between me and the other guys. Most of them aren't Marines. Supposedly SEALS and Rangers, but I don't know if I believe that. Shady from the jump, sir."

They were in a dark and quiet part of the city now, as rundown as Shane's hotel's neighborhood was, but residential. Small, simple houses, and very few lights. Shane drove slowly, trying to not seem suspicious now that he'd finally found a place where his car blended in.

"Why haven't you left the country?" Shane asked. In the backseat, Kat laughed.

"No chance of leaving by plane or train. Copland knows local cops, and they'll have my name and yours on a list by now. Probably have me flagged for something like killing Leclerc. If they catch me, I'm dead. I was trying to plan a route overland on foot when I heard you'd shown up."

"Walk out of Vakovia?" Shane asked.

"Not a lot of other options. Problem is that the nearest city in another country where Copland probably can't reach me before I find a U.S. embassy is maybe Budapest? That's at least one hundred and forty miles, half of it through desolate countryside, forests, and ruins of the last war."

Shane wanted to find Copland, run him down in this ugly car, and be done with it, but it would never be that easy. He was still no closer to understanding why his friend was dead, only that his killer was very thorough and efficient.

"And you sure Copland killed Blakely?" Shane asked then. They had been speaking as though it was obvious, but Shane still didn't see any real motive, and it sounded like Luther didn't, either.

"Positive," Luther replied.

"But why? What's in it for him?"

"Seize the asset, assume control, evaluate, and employ as necessary,"

Kat said in the back seat in a mock masculine voice. Shane glanced at her in the mirror, and she made a face.

"She's right," Luther said. "That's a basic mission brief from Copland for asset recovery. Find something we need, make sure we have control of it, and then use it. That's what he's doing. He's done with Blakely, but he had two men loyal to him who could compromise the mission going forward. He's gone after Leclerc, and I'm next."

"This can't just be about money," Shane said. It was, as far as he could tell, Silvershore's only purpose. They were mercenaries. If Copland was the boss, he got a bigger cut. But was that worth killing three men? Three soldiers?

"It's always about money," Kat said. Luther shook his head.

"Copland's a greedy son of a bitch; you can trust that. I think he would have sold us all out for less than what Silvershore could make on a mission for the right client. But it's whoever put Copland on the map in the first place that we have to worry about. I think it's more than just money for them."

"And you have no idea who that is or what they want," Shane said.

"No, sir."

"Do you know where Blakely died?"

"That, I do know. We all went to get the body. Copland was waiting with him already loaded into a truck. Think maybe he wanted to make a show of it. It's not a place you go alone."

"Bad part of town," Kat said, still playing with her zipper.

"Worse than my hotel?"

The ghost shrugged.

"I'd still want to see it for myself," Shane insisted.

They were now on a pothole-filled road in a part of town dotted with trees and scrub that might have once been farmland. Luther pointed to a dense copse of trees ahead of them in the dark.

"Pull over here," he said.

Shane did as he was told. The car rumbled and sputtered. He turned off the lights and parked on the shoulder of the road.

"This was where Blakely died," the man said, handing Shane a small map that looked like it had come from a gas station. There was a section circled in black ink. "It's called Kogar. Used to be a good-sized city, now it's mostly rubble and ruins. The official word is that Blakely was meeting with rebels, the opposition to President Janosik. The leader's name is Peter Zemba. I don't think he was ever there. Never got word that the rebels were this close to Ravjek."

Shane nodded. Vakovian politics were volatile. The entire region was volatile, and any upheaval could cause a lot of problems. But any time a ruling party was overthrown, there were winners and losers.

"Copland said Blakely insisted on a more diplomatic solution to the problem. Was Silvershore hired to stop Zemba and whatever rebellion he leads? Keep Janosik's control of the country?"

"This guy's good. You should write Tom Clancy novels," Kat said without looking up.

"Threat assessment, and, if necessary, elimination. We'd been stonewalled tracking the rebels down for a long time. Hard to kill a man you can't find. I'm not sure how or when Blakely was supposed to have discovered Zemba so they could have the meeting. I don't think he ever contacted him."

"So, someone wants Janosik to stay in power, and his opposition is killing American consultants out here trying to negotiate a diplomatic end to the fighting, then that makes them look like the villains. They don't want peace, they want bloodshed."

Luther grunted and looked at Kat. She had stopped playing with her zipper but said nothing.

"You can't trust Vakovian media, but there are stories every month or so. Rebels blowing up small settlements, killing civilians by accident when trying to target the military. They've been painting them as villains for a while. Blakely's death was the first one to get any international media attention."

"Blakely and Leclerc died to keep Janosik in power for someone's benefit. Who's got the President of Vakovia in their pocket?" Shane wondered.

Luther shook his head.

"Your guess is as good as mine, but I'm out of this one. This is big, sir. Bigger than two Marines by the side of the road in a garbage VW."

"Where are you headed now?"

"Budapest is that way," Luther said, pointing through the trees. "I was already out of the city when I came back to find you. I have a few contacts I can trust. Someone saw you at my apartment, so I thought you might need a hand. But the best I can offer you is a way out, even though I know you will not take it."

"You're right, I won't," Shane agreed. "But I appreciate it."

Luther held out his hand, and Shane took it.

"Kogar is not safe. The city's dead. I won't tell you not to go but… watch your back, sir," he said.

"You do the same," Shane advised.

"His back is fine; that's what I'm here for," Kat added.

Shane watched them leave from the driver's seat. Neither one looked back as they faded into the woods. Shane turned his attention back to the map he'd been given. He was closer to answers now, but nothing solid. Nothing he could prove. He needed to see where Blakely died.

And he needed to find the ghost his friend had been partnered with.

CHAPTER 11
WHERE DEATH WAITS

Kogar was miles outside of Ravjek. Shane followed the map he'd been provided. There was nothing he could go back for in the city, and no reason to risk his safety trying. The drive was ominous and lonesome, and the Vakovian countryside reminded Shane of war zones he'd been in years before.

The headlights of the car sometimes caught a glimpse of what had once been a farm, now overgrown and falling to pieces. Some of the damage could have been from age, but Shane recognized blast damage when he saw it. Vakovia had been involved in wars in the past, directly and indirectly, but it had been decades as far as Shane knew. This was damage that had never been repaired. The country had never healed or been able to rebuild in any meaningful way after what had happened. The rich built their glass towers in Ravjek, and the poor were cast to the side, or as in the countryside, ceased to exist.

Shane drove for hours. The map showed a direct route that was not workable in real life. Roads did not connect in reality the way they did on the map, and at one point, he had to backtrack for many miles because of a crater in the road that he could not make his way around.

Along with the ruins of farmhouses, the most noticeable thing on the road at night in Vakovia was the dead. Like Ravjek, ghosts roamed the land beyond the city in great numbers.

Some ghosts looked like the lost souls he saw in the oldest cemeteries back home. Their faces were blank, and it was though they couldn't even see him. They walked toward unknown destinations, a process they probably repeated night after night after night.

Others were not so lost. He saw the victims of war, the ghosts of those who had been home when the bombs were dropped or when soldiers rolled through. Many of them were assemblages of ruined parts, walking testaments to suffering. They were burned and broken, dismembered, and torn apart. They existed in the state in which they had died, their torment on display for all time.

Some of these ghosts watched Shane pass with keen interest. It was clear that few people traveled these ruined back roads of Vakovia at night. This was why it was an unusual place for Blakely to be. It seemed the ruined lands behind the capital city were inhospitable and unwanted. Places the ruling classes had decided to sweep aside and ignore. There was nothing leading toward Kogar but death.

Ironically, death had allowed life to claim what was left behind. The ruins were grown over, and the forests and shrubs and crops that had been left were now in charge of the land. There were fields of wheat and barley, and other plants that were harder to identify, crops that had grown wild and been reclaimed by nature just waiting for someone to come and take them once more. Maybe someday people would. But not yet.

When Shane finally got near Kogar, there were not even visible ruins. There was either scrubland or reclaimed farmland and emptiness all around.

He could see places where homes had been even when no ruins remained. The ghosts still clustered there, probably rooted to their remains or treasured possessions, together as families even in the afterlife. He wondered if any of them found that a comfort or if it was more of a curse to be there with their parents and siblings and children. Dead together, forever, in a place that was no longer their home.

Other ghosts were solitary figures. More than one waited for him in the road. They were trying to slow him or stop him entirely, like old urban legends of phantom hitchhikers in America. One was a man who appeared in the headlights only a few yards ahead of the car. Shane didn't swerve or slow, he simply drove through the spirit, catching only the quickest glimpse of surprise on the dead man's face when he realized Shane was willing to run him down.

Later, a woman on the side of the road was weeping, tears streaking makeup down her face, as she reached out and begged for Shane to pull over and take her to safety. Another driver might have fallen for the ruse, but he could see that she was dead.

Maybe she was just looking for companionship, someone to talk to for a mile down the road before she vanished. Or maybe she had a ditch full of victims in the darkness. Either way, Shane had no time or interest in discovering her motives.

The closer he got to Kogar, the slower he had to go. Mists rolled in off the empty fields, obscuring the road ahead. He knew this was all spirit-related, a sign of what was to come. Kat had said that Kogar was a bad part of town. She was not being sarcastic. There was something bad about the place beyond what Luther and the ghost had told him.

Luther said that Kogar was dead, and it was clear what that meant. But Blakely had been found there, either killed on site or dumped there to make it look like it was where he died. Either way, it was something Shane needed to investigate. If the place was as dead as Luther led him to believe, then there would be witnesses. Ghosts, but witnesses, nonetheless.

The air in the car had grown cold, and it set Shane on edge. Vakovia had been stiflingly hot since he'd arrived, an unexpected heatwave that would not relent. For the land around Kogar to be so cold...

Shane had been to ghost towns before. True ghost towns. He and Herbert had nearly been destroyed in a place called Burkitt, Delaware, that had been home to hundreds of spirits. But there was something very different about what he was driving into, he just couldn't put his finger on it.

Based on the map, he guessed that he was close to the city, but there was no signage on any of the roads, so it was hard to tell. With the backtracking he'd done, and the changes in speed to deal with rough roads, and now the mist, he could have been on the outskirts of town or ten miles from it.

The mist thickened to where Shane's headlights were more of a hindrance than a help. The light was scattered in the white haze and created an opaque curtain that reflected at him, blanking out the road. He turned them off and drove blind in the dark, using the scant light from a crescent moon in a cloudy night sky to see.

Figures moved with him in the dark. He could see quick, inconsistent flickers of motion from the corners of his eyes as he slowed the car to a crawl. Some of the craters he had seen on other roads were the size of buildings. The artillery that had blanketed Vakovia must have been powerful to cause such damage. He didn't want to risk driving into a hole he'd never be able to get out of.

A ghost came to the passenger door, a young girl in her mid-teens with half of her face missing. She pressed her hands to the glass and stared in at him as though observing an animal at the zoo. A moment later, she was gone.

Others risked coming into view, either from boldness or out of genuine curiosity. None came at him with aggression, and from the looks of their simple clothes, he suspected these were farmers. He wasn't sure how many even noticed he could see them as he paid little mind to their presence, so concerned was he with staying on the road and not getting into an accident.

The mist was a byproduct of the spirits, a combined affectation more than a conscious effort. There were so many of them together that they were able to affect the environment. They kept the world obscure and ethereal, a danger to any who ventured into it.

Most of the ghosts were probably docile, or at least he hoped they were. In his experience, most would be. But others were not. Aggressive, angry, and powerful spirits would be waiting in the mist. In Kogar. They would be the ones waiting to see who Shane was and what he was doing before they made themselves known.

The mist thickened and Shane slowed more. Something in the murk tapped on the passenger door, but he saw nothing when he looked. It was quick and pointed, like a single fingertip tapping three times.

He kept the car moving at a crawl, and the tapping came again, on the roof this time. It ended with a scraping noise, like something sharp being dragged across the metal, scraping the paint.

Shane checked the mirrors and hit the brakes cautiously. The red lights at the rear of the car saturated the mist, casting the world behind the car in a haze of bloody red. In the distance, outlined in the light, a dark figure rushed toward the car.

He stopped the vehicle and took his foot off the brake. Darkness overwhelmed the car, and he lost sight of his pursuer. Seconds passed, and he waited for it to emerge, but nothing did. He grunted and opened the door.

The cold mist clung to Shane's face as he got out of the vehicle. He took one of the bags from the back seat with him, slung it over his shoulder, and pulled another cigarette from his pack.

Shapes moved in the mist, darting, and circling about him. He flicked the wheel on the lighter and shielded it from the moist air, having to try a second and third time before a flame sparked to life.

Once the cigarette was lit, he exhaled into the mist and took a few cautious steps forward. Three paces ahead of the car, the road fell away into a crater full of rocks and dirt. Weeds grew among the piles of stone, showing it had been in that state for some time. If he'd hit the gas to escape the pursuing shape, as he assumed had been the ghost's intent, he would have crashed into the pit.

Inhospitable, Shane thought. He dropped the duffel bag he'd taken from the car and left it by the hole's edge, hidden by some weeds in a place where it would be easy to find later if he needed it. He didn't want it left in the car where it would be easier for others to find. He then walked the edge of the crater until he was back on the road.

The faint light of the moon cut through the clouds again, and Shane could make out shapes now. Not spirits, but buildings. Concrete structures were collapsed onto one another, some of them substantial in size. They were not the skyscrapers and office buildings of downtown Ravjek, but they must have been good-sized apartment buildings at one point. Ten stories, maybe twelve. They had been people's homes until they were bombed. Now they were ruins, great heaps of rebar and stone and dust.

Here, too, nature had returned. Small trees grew between some of the piles, and swarms of weeds and ivy were visible in the light, obscured by mist. There was no way to know how big Kogar had been or how many people had lived there, but it was a city once. The size of the ruins told Shane the place had to have been home to thousands. And no one had come back. No one had rebuilt. It was gone now. All that remained were the dead and the wreckage that were once their homes.

In the nearest rubble, the spirits moved like bees in a nest, swarming the place. There were hundreds of them.

No one had evacuated the city before it was destroyed. Either no one knew or there was no time. Either way, the people of Kogar had died where they lived. Now, they were chained in place, tied to where they died in massive numbers, their collective trauma a breeding ground for the crossover from life to death.

Shane was surrounded by the dead.

CHAPTER 12
KILLING GROUND

The whispering started so slowly that Shane almost didn't notice. It came from far away at first and was like the sound of a breeze in tall grass, just a faint rustling, no more than background noise. By the time he noticed the words, he wasn't even sure how long he'd been hearing it.

"Ideš zomriet."

It was more than one. Not in harmony, not a chorus, just one and then another, and then another. A handful at first, but then, over time, he could pick out more and more. A dozen voices, and then perhaps two dozen, all waiting their turn to whisper the same message through the mist.

The general meaning was as clear as day. He was not welcome in Kogar. Nothing living was. They were leaving him be for now, but he did not think their grace would last long. It only took one spirit with a taste for blood. Others would join to sate their long-held rage. Some would even do it just because they were bored. With this many ghosts who had died in such violent ways, he knew it was only a matter of time.

"A man died here recently," Shane said to the dark mist.

He was walking slowly, pebbles crunching underfoot as he continued down the main road into the city.

"He was shot. Maybe here, or maybe they dumped his body. He wasn't alone. He would have had a ghost with him, one who was burned."

The spirits continued their whispering, ignoring his words. He watched as they crept across the ruins of buildings on both sides of the road. They were just shapes to him, silhouettes in the dark with the faintest moonlight giving them life.

"Men came and took his body away. Soldiers. Maybe the same ones who killed him, I don't know. I just want to know what happened. Who killed him, how he died. What they said. Someone must have seen something."

Based on the sheer number of spirits in the city, Shane was surprised that Copland, or whoever had done it, had killed Blakely there. They could all see spirits. Did they not think so many witnesses was a risk, even if they were all dead?

"It wasn't here," a ghost said, creeping closer than the others. His accent was thick, but the words were English.

"He wasn't killed here?"

"No," the spirit replied, coming close enough for Shane to see. He was an old man, his skin as white as the mist, as were his hair and eyes. There was no sign of trauma on him, and Shane suspected he had died before the bombings that killed many of the others.

"Where, then?"

"To the east, by the dam and the hydro plant. Quiet there. Hidden away and secret from prying eyes."

The ghost pointed beyond the ruined building and the swarm of spirits to a darkness that showed no sign of any dam or plant to Shane's eyes.

"You saw him die?" Shane asked.

The ghost shook his head.

"None of us go there. That was the *Masaker na Čiernej Rieke*," the ghost said. "The Black River Massacre. It was before the bombs, when Colonel Toth arranged to meet his counterparts from the three other factions in the war. He invited them to meet at the plant, the source of all power in the region before the Chekov nuclear plant was finished, to come to an amicable decision over power distribution. Instead, he killed them all where they stood."

"An ambush," Shane said. "Under the guise of peace."

"Yes. But no peace. Just deception and death. The spirits there all had black hearts before those here were doomed to join them. We are not welcome there. No one is."

"The ghosts there saw what happened to my friend," Shane said, though it did not come out as a question.

"If anyone did. But they would have killed him themselves. Like they will kill you if you go."

Shane looked around the mist. The movement had all but stopped. There were silhouettes like a crowd of spectators all around him and the pale, old man. Hundreds of figures of all shapes and sizes.

"How did you know he was here if you didn't see?" Shane asked.

"We know. Nothing with blood flowing through its veins can enter Kogar without us knowing," the ghost replied. His tone was not as dark as the words he spoke, but it struck Shane as something ominous, nonetheless.

The ghosts and the mist were working together in the city. He wondered if there was some kind of shared awareness among them, a perception that had grown beyond the individual. Could ghosts work like that? Like some kind of hive when their numbers grew so high? Or maybe it had to do with their shared fate. Or maybe the old man was just being darkly poetic.

"Appreciate the help," Shane said. He headed east in the direction the ghost had indicated. The whispers in the mist grew louder, more urgent, and more anxious.

"You will die, American," the old man said, not joining him.

"I wouldn't count on it," Shane replied. If there were witnesses, he'd find out what had happened to Blakely and then deal with it accordingly.

The mist seemed to part around Shane as he walked. The ghosts kept their distance, and he was able to mostly follow roads as he headed toward the old power plant. Much of the old infrastructure was destroyed and buried, and at times, he had to climb over and around rubble to find his way. The pavement had been blasted to gravel in some places, and so had the buildings. At one point, he climbed through what remained of someone's living room, oddly preserved but on its side in the debris.

Killing Blakely in the same way and in the same place as others had been duped in the past was no accident. It made Shane doubt Copland's control of the situation. Copland was American, and this sounded very much like a dark joke from someone who knew their Vakovian history.

President Janosik might not have had a hand in getting Copland in charge of Silvershore, or the forming of the company, but he had to be the client. If not him, then someone on his behalf. Under the circumstances, it was too much of a coincidence that his opponent was being thrown under the bus for Blakely's death.

The mist grew colder, and clouds covered the moon. The silhouettes in the darkness vanished, becoming part of the shadows. Shane was alone in the black as he plodded onward, climbing over and through the rubble.

He was nearly through another collapsed apartment when a rock gave way underfoot and a wall collapsed. He slipped down to the road and landed on his backside. The fall was only six or seven feet, but the wall on which he'd been balancing crumbled. It allowed more rubble to spill out with it, including bits of glass and wood and metal.

Shane could see broken glass and crockery and bent pieces of tableware like forks and spoons. Someone's kitchen had tumbled from the debris, and with it, a single human skull rolled next to his hand where he'd fallen.

He stared down at the fleshless face. It was covered in a thick layer of dust, and it was small. Much smaller than an adult's. The rest of the body was missing, still somewhere under the stone and steel.

Shane touched the skull lightly, and it was like ice. He pulled his hand away and looked into the darkness. The ghost of a child crouched at his feet. A little girl, maybe Eloise's age. Her limbs were bent in too many places, the bones broken, and she was covered in the same dust as her skull.

"*Kto si?*" the spirit whispered.

"My name is Shane."

"*Nie je to tu bezpečné,*" she continued.

It is not safe here... Shane translated in his head.

There was earnestness in her tone, and deep sadness as well. The dust was like flour, caked onto nearly every inch of her. It was dark around her eyes and nose and mouth, where tears and blood had soaked it and made it muddy.

Shane got slowly to his feet as she watched, shifting back on her haunches to get out of his way.

"They kill," the girl said in halting, harsh English. She pointed in the direction that he was headed.

"I know," he said with a nod. "I'll be okay."

"No," she disagreed, shaking her head. "*Pridáte sa k nám.*"

It was a warning; he would die if he continued. Her eyes were wide beneath the gray dust that covered her.

He left the girl behind and continued through the darkness. The destruction lessened as he traveled several more blocks. The larger buildings vanished and some of the smaller ones were still half standing.

Soon enough, the whispering in the mist took on a new tone. A constant rushing sound. It was not the words of the dead now; it was the sound of water. He was approaching a fast-moving river, and the sound grew louder and louder. By the time he could see what he was approaching, the noise was all but deafening.

The hydroelectric plant on the Black River was enormous, an immense beast of Cold War-era construction made of concrete that spanned one shore of the massive river to the other. The gates had been left open or destroyed, and the water rushed through the other side as a deafening waterfall. Even in the scant light, Shane could see the mist clouds that rose from the unseen depths on the north side of the plant.

There were a handful of ruined buildings on the same side of the river on which Shane found himself, but the bulk of the structure was the dam. It was large enough to drive cars across in two lanes and featured four tall, concrete towers evenly placed across the distance. Whether the towers controlled the gates, were for observation, or something else, Shane did not know.

He could hear nothing above the roar. From the ruined road where Shane stood, it was like the never-ending cry of a beast in the shadows. He could not see the water flow yet—it was too dark, and he was not in the right position—but it consumed everything.

That a river could flow endlessly in such a torrent was almost as shocking as everything else he had seen in the city. The ruins, the spirits, everything about Kogar was awe-inspiring and terrifying.

Shane was alone, with no silhouettes in the mist and no shadows pacing his progress. Despite the warning he'd received from the pale old man, nothing was waiting for him in the dark at the plant. And that, of course, put him on edge even more.

In the heart of Kogar, the ghosts were all the doomed souls who died in someone else's war, civilian casualties of careless bombing. But the spirits at the Black River were those of the betrayed, if the story was true. Souls gathered under false pretenses and killed for someone else's gain.

"I want to ask about the man who was shot here," Shane said loudly, but his words were drowned by the roaring water.

No one answered, and no one appeared. If the dead would not appear, then Shane would have to find them.

He headed for the ruined buildings.

CHAPTER 13
IN THE DEAFENING DARKNESS

The nearest building to Shane looked like it might have been an administrative office rather than something that dealt with anything technical related to the dam or the electrical plant. It was small, and there was evidence of a parking lot outside, now shattered and strewn with the rubble of the building.

The bombs had not hit the dam, but they had come close. The structural integrity must have been compromised, and Shane wondered how safe the dam was after all these years. Maybe that was why the water still flowed, though. Perhaps the gates had been damaged beyond repair and nothing could hold back the river.

A road, still driveable, cut across the space between Shane and the parking lot. Perhaps it was how Blakely arrived and got to the spot, and how they took his body away when he was dead. There was no proper place for the living to meet in seclusion unless they wanted to risk entering half-destroyed buildings. Whoever Blakely thought he was meeting would have had to meet him where all the dead could see.

"His name was Davis Blakely. I'm told he was invited here to talk. To try to make peace with someone. And they shot him instead," Shane said. He could barely hear himself above the water, but the dead would hear him. He just hoped they understood.

He approached the building and crossed the road into the lot out front. The shadows in the half-collapsed entryway coalesced and scuttled toward him.

The ghost was not upright; it crawled using its hands while the legs dragged uselessly behind it. The weak moonlight was barely enough for Shane to see that the ghost did not have legs below the knees. Instead, it trailed splintered bone, ragged flesh, and scraps of the pants it once wore. The blood trail still looked fresh, and the deep red reflected the light.

When the ghost was close enough, Shane could see its face. He was a balding man, with most of the flesh from his face torn away in small, scattered slices. Shrapnel had torn him to pieces. His clothes were blood-soaked rags all over, and through the holes, Shane could see more exposed flesh, muscle, and bone.

The ghost moved painfully slowly, crawling, and dragging himself from the fallen entrance of the building across the busted parking lot, dark eyes locked on Shane the entire time.

"Did you see my friend die?" Shane asked as the bloody, broken body lurched toward him. The ghost's mouth hung slack, frothy blood bubbling and dripping as he wheezed and groaned with each strained movement. His ragged hands dug into the stone, found purchase, and pulled another few inches closer. His gaze never wavered.

Shane waited for him to get close. He watched the ghost's ruined face twist into an expression of malice, and it reached for him with a ruined and bloody hand, the fingers bent at awkward angles, and the nails peeled back and crusted with black scabs.

"Tell me what happened," Shane demanded, crouching to meet the ghost, and catching hold of him before he could touch Shane. His hands curled into the ghost's bloody, shredded shirt and lifted him off the ground. Devoid of most of his legs, he was two-thirds of his normal height.

Shane held him up like he was a child, using the moment of shock that registered on the ghost's face over being manhandled by a living human to hold him close to his face and look the spirit in the eyes.

"Did you see a man get shot here?"

"What are you?" the ghost croaked, barely audible over the falls. His accent was Slovakian, but his English was clear, even if his voice sounded breathless from the holes that must have been torn through his lungs by the shrapnel.

"Just a guy looking for some answers," Shane explained.

"I don't understand this," the ghost continued. It wasn't Shane's question that confused him, it was Shane. He did not understand how Shane could touch him or hold him up as he did. The implications of what else Shane might do had to have been running through his mind.

A second spirit hobbled from the shadows of the building. It was upright and in possession of its legs, but the blast that had killed it had torn its body nearly in half. The ghost's torso was split apart, exposing ribs and internal organs. There was no right side at all, just a great chasm from hips all the way to head. Even the side of the ghost's neck had been torn away. Everything on the right side of the head was gone a fraction of an inch past the nose. Just half a mouth, a single eye, and a crushed skull exposing the brain within.

The ghost walked with a staggered, meandering gait. It drifted left then right as if correcting itself with each step. The one eye in its head, bloodshot and intense, was fixed on Shane and the ghost he held in his grasp.

A third ghost appeared, this one nearly skinless and embedded with shards of stone from head to toe. Another joined it, his body bent nearly in half and crushed almost flat, the bones underneath jutting through torn and deeply bruised flesh.

Each of the spirits had died in a violent explosion. The pale ghost said it was before the bombing. They must have been lured to the building, which was rigged to blow once they were inside.

"Who killed the man who was shot here? What was said?" Shane demanded of the ghost he held up.

"It does not matter," the ghost muttered, more blood sputtering from his lips. "You will join him now."

"I can leave here peacefully," Shane pointed out. "You can make this easy."

The ghost laughed, no longer enamored with Shane's ability to physically interact with him. He lifted his arms, grasping Shane's wrists in his hands as ghostly blood sputtered from his mouth. The spray coated Shane's face, cold, sticky, and so real he could almost taste the salty, metallic tang.

"There is no peace here," the spirit said through the laughter.

Shane hurled the ghost aside as the half-man approached, shambling like a drunk with his one arm outstretched and his single eye full of hate. The ghost did not have enough of a mouth to speak; instead, it made gurgling sounds that rose from its ruined chest cavity.

The ghost made a play for Shane, trying to grab him with one hand. Shane parried and took the ghost by the wrist, pulling it off-balance. He yanked the stumbling figure toward himself and then dragged it back two steps onto the road and out of the parking lot.

"I came to talk," Shane said to the others coming at him. "But we can do this if you want."

The ghost was already missing half a head. It had no defenses. If it couldn't speak and seemed intent on attacking Shane, then there was no need to keep it around.

Shane reached into the ghost's open skull, bracing the body with his other hand. He grasped the edges of the bone, his fingers plunging into the gore that had once been the ghost's brain, and he pulled.

A crack sounded like thin wood breaking, and the ghost's head broke and pulled apart. He held his form just long enough to produce a surprise groan before the ghostly body exploded.

Shane turned his head from the blast and braced himself. A rush of pressure lasted for a blink of an eye and then was gone, the ghost along with it.

The legless ghost stared wide-eyed at Shane from the ground, and the others stopped their approach. Shane watched them all, keeping his eyes open for others who might advance from the darkness, shielded by the noise of the falls.

"Tell me about the man who died," Shane demanded.

"He was there," the legless ghost answered, pointing to nothing. "He died there."

Shane walked several paces away and looked back. The ghost nodded. The others held their ground but did not come closer after seeing their companion destroyed.

The cement at Shane's feet was stained dark. He crouched and lowered his hand. It was dry, but there was a tackiness to it. A bloodstain, a large one, covered the pavement. At least five or six pints spilled. And drag marks as well.

He followed the path of two large arches, maybe boot heels that were dragged through the blood when it was fresh. Someone had lifted a body, pulled it forward, and then plucked it from the ground.

Blakely had been killed there. He had gone to Kogar for something. Maybe he really thought he was meeting with the opposition leader. Hell, maybe he had met him for real, and the man was working with Copland. But Blakely had died there.

"What happened?" Shane asked.

The legless ghost slowly crawled closer but kept his distance from Shane this time.

"This man came with another. He came with the dead, a burned man. They talked. They approached the building. He did not know a man had come earlier. A man waited for him."

"This man killed him?" Shane asked.

"No," the ghost answered. "The burned ghost did. He watched the living man approach until there, where you stand. And then he hit the man in the back when the waiting man appeared. He pushed his hand through the man's chest. He pulled his heart from the hole."

Shane looked down at the stain. Blakely's heart had been torn from his chest.

"What about the man who was already here?"

"He watched. He took photos. Then took the body in the man's car and left with the ghost."

"Describe him."

"Older than the man that died. Very tall. Scarred mouth," the ghost replied.

Shane nodded. Copland. He didn't kill Blakely; he simply watched. He had Blakely's partner do the work, to take him by surprise. There had not been a meeting with the opposition. Whether Blakely thought that's who he was meeting didn't matter. It didn't happen. He was betrayed by both of his partners, living and dead.

"You watched all of it?" Shane asked.

"Watched. And rejoiced," the legless ghost said spitefully. Shane glared at the thing. He could reach him in just a few paces. He could lift him from the ground again and crush his head like he was made of trash. He could destroy them all, the ragged lot of already broken monstrosities.

"Kogar is for the dead," the ghost said. "Only the dead deserve it."

"It's yours," Shane retorted. "Keep it. Forever."

He stood up, looking at the blood at his feet. The ghost had hit Blakely in the back. Didn't even let him know he'd been betrayed. He'd killed him like a coward, and Copland just watched it happen. He took pictures of it so he could have proof of what happened. And for what? To pin the blame on some faceless enemy and ensure a paycheck for the Reaper Company?

Lights flashed in the darkness and Shane turned quickly as a pair of headlights came into view up the road from his position, a second pair right behind. There was no reason for anyone to be on that road at that time. The drive in had shown him that no one drives to Kogar, at least not at night. Unless they had a specific reason to.

Shane ran back to the ruins of the city. He didn't know how they'd tracked him, but Reaper Company had found him.

He needed to find cover in a city full of the dead.

Chapter 14
Breaking Spirits

Bullets zipped past Shane's head, peppering slabs of broken concrete, and causing tiny, explosive bursts of shrapnel to embed in his flesh as he ducked below the wall of a collapsed building.

The sound of gunfire echoed through the ruins, bouncing off toppled walls until it sounded like a dozen guns. He crawled through the remains of broken homes and kept his head down, moving from one precarious pile of rubble to the next.

He hadn't seen the number of pursuers, but there were two SUVs. He guessed there were at least eight mercenaries and likely their ghost companions. Sixteen members of Reaper Company were on him, fully armed and intent on killing him. He was armed with a Marine Kabar, a pair of iron knuckles, and nothing else.

The whispering dead filled the ruins, silhouettes in the endless mist, in a frenzy as they watched the hunt unfold. With no knowledge of the lay of the land, Shane would have been at a disadvantage even in a normal city. But this place, with its ruins and malevolent spirits, was nearly impossible to navigate.

He darted deeper into the city, keeping as low and quiet as he could. The fading roar of the falls and the whispering of spirits covered much of the noise he made. The living would have to take their time trying to keep up, but the dead would have far fewer limitations. If eight spirits were in pursuit, Shane would need more than just noise to help him survive.

Shane pulled the iron knuckles from his pocket and slipped them on, heading over the remains of another destroyed apartment building and then around the crater of the bomb that had leveled it. He was only a couple of blocks past where he had encountered the pale, old ghost that had directed him to the dam, but he was already deeper into the destruction than he thought possible. What he had seen was just the outer edges. The true devastation, even obscured in the mist and darkness, rivaled those he had seen during his time in the Marines.

The city had been absolutely destroyed with no quarter given to those who had lived there. Skeletal remains were scattered beneath his feet alongside the fractured pieces of walls and homes and once-lived lives.

He had never heard of what happened in Kogar. There were no stories shared alongside the list of historical atrocities laid at the feet of past empires that accounted for what he was seeing. War crimes had been committed in the city. An entire population had been wiped out, and Shane had never heard a whisper about it.

Maybe that's why Blakely is dead, Shane thought. Maybe someone hired the Reapers to deal with the political opposition in Vakovia and Blakely found out why the opposition was fighting, and what the people in charge had kept under wraps for however many years it had been. Maybe someone paid Copland to make sure the dead stayed buried in the ruins of their homes.

Ghosts were huddled under half-fallen walls and shattered floors. They perched on the remnants and crept from behind as Shane made his way around the largest bomb crater he'd seen so far and ducked into what remained of a building, now just three floors and a crumbled foundation next to the toppled higher stories that were spread about the streets below.

The interior of the darkened building was as cold as any winter night back in Nashua. Ghosts filled the space, packed nearly shoulder to shoulder. He pushed through them and backed against the wall nearest the entrance, pausing to catch his breath.

Dozens of eyes watched him as the whispers continued. He watched the dead watching him, waiting for any to make a move, but none did.

They were as curious as he was, it seemed, to find out what happened next.

Shane could hear nothing from outside in the mist. The whispering was a ceaseless background noise, but there was no sound of pursuit yet. Not that he expected the Reapers to announce their arrival, but he strained to hear any sign of someone approaching, even the scraping of a boot or rubble shifting position.

Minutes ticked by and he held his position, breathing slowly and evenly while the clustered ghosts watched as though they were statues. The whispering grew quieter, and one ghost, a teenage boy, raised a hand and pointed to the door with his eyes still on Shane.

There were no footfalls because there were no feet. A ghost drifted in the door, his legs ending in the mist that covered the floor. He was dressed in rags, and his flesh was the color of rancid meat. Shane had seen him briefly in the lot next to the Silvershore building. He was partnered with one of the mercenaries.

The rotten ghost had one good eye and one that drooped under a saggy eyelid. His face looked like it was threatening to slip from the skull beneath it at any moment. Shane waited for him to fully enter the room.

He lunged at the ghost, but it was more agile than it appeared. His iron-lined fist was knocked aside, and the knuckles flew from his grip as the ghost caught him and then fell to the ground in the doorway, holding Shane by the wrists.

The wild eyes of the rotting spirit were wide as he let out a cackle. Shane's forehead met the ghost's face, and he cut the laughter short as he broke the spirit's nose and split open his lip.

There was no time to finesse the situation or gather intel. The ghost would have nothing useful to offer, anyway. Shane drove a knee into the spirit's groin, forcing him to release his grip and recoil.

Shane plunged his thumbs into the ghost's eyes. It wailed as Shane lifted and then slammed the rotten head into the ground with all the force he could muster.

Bone crunched and squelched. A second blow caused the head to collapse entirely as Shane rolled aside to escape the brunt of the blast that followed. The ghost was destroyed, the force of the blow causing the spirits in the room to surge backward like a wave.

The whispering stopped. Somewhere in the mist, a man cried out in pain. He had kept the haunted item too close and suffered an injury as the destruction of the spirit caused the destruction of the item. Maybe not a fatality, but Shane would take a wounding and consider it a win.

The ghosts in the room with Shane had gone silent. Outside, they had followed suit. Kogar was truly like a grave now. The spirits watched him, not with the same detached, blank disinterest they had before. There was something else now. Fear, maybe. Or awe. Something akin to what the legless ghost at the dam had displayed.

Shane retrieved the iron knuckles from where they'd fallen and slipped them back onto his hand. He'd be better served destroying ghosts for now if he could rather than sending them back to their living partners with the knowledge of where he was hidden. But he needed to survive long enough to escape, and that meant getting away however he could.

A second ghost entered the ruins, one Shane did not recognize. It was a beast of a man, wide-shouldered with a wild beard and bullet holes spread across his bare chest. A bullet hole in his head bled into one eye as he scanned the room. Shane backed toward a corner, sizing up his new opponent. The ghost looked like a professional wrestler, nearly all muscle beneath the series of wounds that had killed him.

"I've been looking forward to this, mate," the ghost said joyfully. He spoke with an Australian accent, and his face broke into a genuine smile of delight.

The ghost broke into a run, covering the handful of steps between himself and Shane. He ducked low and buried a shoulder in Shane's gut, slamming him into the wall before picking him up and throwing him back across the room as though he weighed nothing.

Shane hit the ground hard, his vision spinning as his skull hit a rock. He shook his head to clear it as the big man came at him again, blood pouring from his many wounds.

Instead of trying to dodge, Shane launched himself at the ghost. His fist made contact with the spirit's chin, a quick jab with the iron knuckles, and the ghost was banished back to his haunted item and the mercenary that carried it.

Shane ran from the ruins. There was no way to know how far away the ghost was or how much time he'd bought himself. The position was compromised, though, and he needed new cover.

He slipped and scuttled across loose stone and debris. Somewhere behind him, something collapsed loudly in a testament to the dangers all around them and a mercenary screamed in pain. Shane smirked and kept going, leading them deeper into the dangers of the bombed city. He would employ any advantage he could find that would take them out.

A gun fired, and Shane heard the bullet zip past his head, pinging off something metal in the dark. He dropped lower and changed direction, pushing through crowds of spirits that stood in the ruins and watched. If all members of Reaper Company could see ghosts, then he could use the spirits as cover as easily as he could use the shattered buildings.

Men called out to each other, trying to pinpoint Shane's position and close in on him. He ducked into another building, smaller than the others and still relatively intact.

The second floor had collapsed onto the first, and Shane had to climb across the uneven floor toward a window on the far side that led to an alley. Bodies were slumped under piles of stone and metal, mostly skeletal now, long forgotten after the city's destruction.

"You'll die here with us."

The voice was familiar, and Shane saw the pale ghost he had first met creep from under a fallen support beam.

"Maybe," Shane said, racing past the spirit and out the window into the alley. The Reapers were closing in fast, and he had little time to entertain doomsayers.

One building had fallen against another in the alley, creating an ominous passageway underneath them. It would be an excellent place to lay a trap if Shane had any explosives handy, but he did not. Instead, it would serve as minimal cover and nothing more.

He ran under the half-fallen building. Above his head, ghosts stared down out of windows angled to face the ground. He ignored them and cleared the potential danger zone, coming out of the alley and onto a new street lined with overturned and burned-out cars.

Shane took cover behind a car that was on its side, windows long since smashed out, and the interior rotten from years of exposure to the elements.

"There is no place to go."

The pale, old man had returned. He was crouched by the vehicle's trunk. Shane scowled and was about to say something less than polite when his eyes fell on the tire iron at the ghost's side, half-covered in weeds growing from the shattered pavement. It was not a high-powered rifle, but it was better than nothing.

Shane pulled the tire iron free and ran to the next car, staying low, and searching for signs of movement.

"Kogar demands death," the ghost said, catching up to him again.

Shane sighed and shook his head.

"If you're that hungry to kill something, kill the ones chasing me," he said.

The old ghost's face split into a smile and he laughed, the sound merging with the whispers.

"Excellent idea," he said, fading into the shadows of the city.

Chapter 15

Setting the Snare

Shane could hear yelling between mercenaries close to his position. He was crouched in the weeds, using another destroyed car for cover, and waiting for a chance to make a move.

At least two members of Reaper Company were on the same street with him, but he had only seen one. There was no sign of the ghosts that had to be with them as well, so he was staying low and watching.

The ghosts of Kogar had receded, and the whispering had ceased. It made the place even more unnerving to Shane. At least when they were assembled and whispering around him, there were no surprises and no doubts about the city. That had changed.

Shane heard stones crunching under boots as one mercenary drew closer. From his position in the weeds, Shane could see the man's face as he paced slowly down the street, holding his rifle at the ready. He was one of the soldiers Shane saw when he staked out the Silvershore office.

A radio crackled quietly, and the soldier pressed a button on his vest.

"Copy that," he whispered, drawing closer to Shane's position.

Shane squeezed the tire iron tightly. If the soldier discovered him, he might have time to crush the man's skull before he got a shot off. It depended on whether he went left or right around the car Shane was using for cover. He was just a few feet from it and would have to make a choice in seconds.

The soldier reached the rear of the car. If he turned left and looked down, he'd see Shane for sure. Shane tensed, his grip on the tire iron as tight as possible. Sweat beaded on his forehead, and he held his breath.

And then a whisper broke the silence.

"Kemper?" the soldier whispered. He turned on his heels and scanned the street.

The whisper spoke again but Shane could not make out the words. He couldn't even tell what language they were in.

"What?" the mercenary said, raising his voice.

A second whisper joined the first.

"Anyone else hearing this?" the man asked over the radio. Static was his only answer.

"This is Cortez. Where is everyone?" the man said. The radio hissed in reply.

"Kemper!" Cortez yelled, ignoring the radio. He turned in a half-circle just feet from Shane. "Hey, come on, man!"

A third whisper joined. Shane could only see Cortez's feet through the broken rear window of the vehicle. He watched the soldier stop moving and freeze, facing away from Shane.

"Kemper, that you?" he said. Shane could hear no response. Cortez chambered a round in his weapon.

"Stop right there, buddy," he ordered. Shane couldn't see who or what he was aiming at or speaking to.

"Jesus," Cortez said softly, fear plain in his voice. The sound of gunfire filled the darkness. Shane could see the muzzle flare flashing through the shadows and spent rounds falling to the ground. Cortez unloaded an entire clip into the darkness.

The gun clicked, and the man turned and ran. He bolted around the side of the car toward Shane's hiding spot.

Shane stood quickly and pulled back with the tire iron, ready to swing. Cortez's eyes were wide as he caught sight of Shane. In the same instant, Shane watched a looming shadow rise from the darkness behind the mercenary. Arms wrapped around the man's chest and hands like claws dug into the Kevlar. A skeletal face came over his shoulder and bit down on his throat, spraying blood across the ruined car Shane had used as cover.

In an instant, the dark spirit pulled back and up into the nearby ruins, dragging Cortez with it. It was like watching a bird of prey pluck a mouse from a field. The man's screams faded into the whispers, which had returned with a vengeance. Only the spray of blood and some scattered brass bullet casings showed that the man had been there at all.

Gunfire half a block down started and ended abruptly in another scream. More echoed throughout the ruins. Shots, screams, and somewhere, an explosion.

The air grew colder, and Shane ran from his position, backtracking toward where he'd entered the city. The spirits had taken him up on his suggestion and were killing Copland's men.

Whispers followed him as he found the body of the next mercenary. His head had been removed, but not a drop of blood was spilled anywhere. Shane didn't waste time puzzling over it and instead took the weapon off the dead man and a bag he had slung over his shoulder.

Shane ran, and ghosts paced him. Gunfire a block over echoed through the ruins. He could see no one living, but he heard the cries of at least five of the Silvershore mercs. Two were dead for sure, but he suspected the ghosts were not wounding the others. There would be no one left alive in Kogar in a matter of minutes, and he wasn't sure whether that included him.

It was just a few blocks to get back to the crater where he'd parked his car. Shane would be fine if the ghosts kept busy with Reaper Company. He didn't necessarily believe it, but he told himself that.

By the time he reached the edge of the city, the place where he'd first met the pale ghost and the whispering spirits of the mist, he had not heard a scream or a gunshot for at least five minutes.

The ghosts still whispered but kept their distance from him. He saw the pale, old man among them as he left the rubble of Kogar behind, but neither said a word to the other.

Lights appeared in the darkness ahead as an engine ground harshly to life. Shane recognized the sound of his trashy VW. Someone had hotwired it.

He ran around the crater and watched as the car turned around and pulled away. It had to be one of the mercenaries. Shane shouldered the weapon he'd taken from the headless soldier and fired a round into the back of the escaping vehicle. Glass shattered, and the car swerved but righted itself quickly and kept going. The distance was too great and the mist too thick to get another clean shot off. Shane cursed and returned to the crater's edge, retrieving the bag he'd dropped there earlier. There were few choices left. He needed to move, so he kept walking until the mist and whispers faded, and he was in the darkened Vakovian countryside once more.

He could not go back into Kogar. The mercenary who had stolen his car had to have called in to base once he was far enough from the city to safely use his radio again. Copland would come, and Shane was stranded miles from anything. Ravjek was the only option.

Shane pulled a cigarette from the pack and lit it, breathing deeply as the chill of Kogar fell away and he was back in the oppressive heat of the countryside. He looked around at the darkness and then stopped, staring out at nothing. They would track him soon enough. He needed time to devise a plan, and a place to regroup and resupply, and then he'd take the fight to Silvershore and shut them down. He just had to live long enough to do it.

"What a stupid idea," he said to himself as he left the road behind and jogged into the darkness.

✳ ✳ ✳

It was after three in the morning, and Joseph Copland did not want to be in his office. The ghost he knew as Vox paced angrily in the shadows along the wall. His frail, skeletal form made him look terrifying but weak. He was anything but.

Vox was one of the deadliest killers Copland had ever met, and he had met many. The ghost was a sadist, though he was loath to admit he enjoyed anything. It was undeniable, though. Watching him work, watching him torture and kill, was to watch a man at peace with himself. Or something that used to be a man, anyway.

There was but a single radio contact with the team that had left for Kogar. Chief Petty Officer Danny Phan had a panicked message that was relayed to Copland. Reapers down. Target still at large. Mission failure.

Phan was on his way back to the office. Eight men had deployed and only one returned. No one even confirmed contact with Ryan, let alone confirmed a kill.

"You should have let me gut him when he was here," Vox growled from the shadows.

"We all benefit from the clarity of hindsight," Copland said.

He didn't understand how Shane Ryan was such a problem. He was one man. He hadn't been an active Marine in years. But he had a way to kill ghosts, and that was worrisome.

Copland's experiences with the dead went back decades, even before he joined the military. He had seen ghosts as a boy, and he grew up in a home where the ghost of his grandfather lurked in the walls and terrorized him for years. His parents refused to listen to him; his father beat him for "making up stories". And at night, his grandfather crept from the shadows, his flesh rotten and his voice frightening, and would tell Joseph how he would die, a new nightmare every single night.

With age came more understanding, and in time, he developed friendships and then partnerships with spirits like Vox. Ones that could do things for him, and in turn, he did things for them. A symbiotic relationship that benefited everyone.

After all those years, Copland was able to make good on his skill and experience. Not just his time in the military, and not just his experience with and understanding of the dead, but a combination. The money was practically unheard of. He'd be set for the rest of his life—beyond set—in a few years. Able to live in luxury until the day he died, all for moving invisible pieces on a chessboard to let people he couldn't care less about take control of backwater countries like Vakovia.

Shane Ryan stood in the way of all of that, just like Davis Blakely had. The man wanted to work as a mercenary with ethics. It was absurd. His death was a favor to the world. He needed to be removed from the gene pool and Ryan needed to follow, but the man was like a cockroach.

"He's got to be trapping them," Vox hissed. The ghost was certain Ryan could not kill the dead. The dead didn't die. No one else had seen it happen.

"They're not trapped. You saw that mangled metal from Houghton. That wasn't a trap," Copland said to the ghost.

"Some other way. I told you salt works, too. There are tricks. Just tricks!"

As useful as Vox was when it came to killing, he was poor at strategy and worse at conversation. He was single-minded. Cruel and creative, he was a well-trained attack dog and nothing more.

Phan would be back soon enough for a debrief, but Copland wasn't sure the soldier would have any valuable info to help explain Ryan's abilities. He also wasn't convinced he needed it. He'd communicated over the radio that someone had shot at his vehicle. That was Ryan. He was alive. That was all Copland needed to know.

Ryan was in Vakovia for vengeance, and he had not found it. His sights would be set on Copland. They had to be by now. And with nowhere else to go, he would be on the run to one place only: Silvershore.

The man was no coward, that was clear. But stupid? Maybe. Shane had traveled across the world with no idea what he was doing or who he was up against. His strategic thinking was on par with Vox's.

Copland picked up the phone from his desk and pressed a button. The number was a direct line to Ravjek's chief of police.

"Miroslav," Copland said when the man picked up.

"Colonel Copland," the chief replied, his accent thick. "It is very late."

"It is," Copland agreed, "but I have a problem I need you to fix. A criminal at large in your city. Shane Ryan. American. Retired Marine. He's murdered several of my men. I think he works for Zemba."

"I see," the chief said. "Such a dangerous criminal might need to be shot on sight."

"That's probably for the best if your men get the opportunity," Copland said. "I'll send you his photo, you can have it dispersed."

"Understood," the chief said, and the line went dead. Copland would send them Ryan's dossier and add some funds to an account he'd set up for the chief after he'd arrived in Ravjek. It was good to have important people in one's pocket.

"The police?" Vox said disdainfully. "You think they will succeed where your men already failed?"

"No," Copland admitted. "But they will keep Ryan on the run, in the shadows, and on edge. It'll make him easier to find, in time. He has no friends left in Vakovia. He has no money, he has no passport, and now there is no one he can turn to for help. He'll be dead soon enough."

Chapter 16
Surviving the Game

The sun was blazing when Shane awoke. He was hiding in some underbrush in a small copse of trees at the far edge of an abandoned farm property. He had trekked through the night, following rocky paths, small streams, and whatever else he could do to cover his trail and make it all but impossible for anyone to follow him. When he was too exhausted to go farther, he hunkered down for the rest of the night.

He had only slept for a short time. The bright sun and cloying heat ensured it would be impossible to last any longer, which was what he had planned for, anyway. He needed rest, but not that much.

The skyline of Ravjek was already visible in the distance. Shane knew Copland would expect him to return to the city. He could accomplish nothing if he stayed away, and after the colonel had sent the team to kill him in Kogar, there was no way Shane wouldn't be back. Now, he had to stay off the radar, use some misdirection, and keep Copland focused on the wrong things.

Shane hiked back to the city and made his way along side streets and alleyways to the outdoor market, where he picked up a hat, sunglasses, and a plain, white T-shirt with some of the cash he had left. If the ghost in the nightclub knew his face, then everyone attached to Silvershore knew his face. He'd need to stay hidden as best as he could.

What was left of the cash from Luther's apartment after he paid Milos for the car and supplies had been taken along with his passport, so he made his way back to Luther's to take some more. Getting around Ravjek would require money, and Shane had lost everything.

His walk was casual and unrushed. He blended in with the citizens of the city, just another person out on the hot day, enjoying the sun. He walked in the front door of the building like he lived there and made his way to the apartment, the same as he had before.

The door was still unlocked, and he let himself in unnoticed by the neighbor. He moved quickly, snagging another envelope of cash he'd seen on his first visit, and then headed to the bedroom for a second one.

Shane stopped in the doorway. The bedroom was not as he'd left it. Luther's body was splayed out face-down on the bed, a gunshot in the back of his head. There was no splatter pattern, and no blood on the still-made bed. He'd been killed elsewhere and then moved to his home, left there for the police to find. Or maybe for Shane.

He felt the pit of his stomach tighten as a police siren screamed to life in the near distance. It was the same, distant wail he'd heard on his first visit. This one was mere blocks away, alerting the world to its presence just moments from the scene, but far enough away that if someone had walked up to the apartment, they wouldn't have seen anyone lying in wait.

Copland had covered his bases well. Shane cursed and grabbed the money he'd come for, leaving the apartment, and making his way to the stairwell as quickly as he could.

He headed up instead of down as a second siren joined the first. By the time he made it to the roof, four police cars were parked on the street below.

Luther's building was not huge. There were only six floors, but Shane was left with few options now that he was roof-bound. He walked the edge of the building, keeping out of view of the street below as he looked for a way to get down unseen, or at least to one of the neighboring buildings.

"You on a walking tour or something?"

Kat was on the roof with him, hidden next to a clunky, old-school cooling unit that hummed and clanged as the fan inside spun loudly.

"I thought you two left town. What happened?"

"Luther got himself killed. You miss that part?"

The ghost's tone was defensive and angry. There was some genuine feeling there, a sense of loss. If she had taken protecting Luther to heart, then she had failed. As a ghost, she was still bound to her haunted item, which was probably still with him. She couldn't leave even if she wanted to, a further reminder of what went wrong.

"No, I didn't," Shane said.

"Must have had some kind of tracker on him. Maybe during the physical when he first joined up, they tagged him with a chip like a dog at the vet. I don't know. They found us, though. Fight didn't last long."

She looked down, shaking her head, and speaking just barely loud enough to be heard.

"I need help getting out of here," he told the ghost. There was no time to reminisce about Luther or feel bad. Shane had minutes at most.

"What's that got to do with me?" Kat asked. "Luther's dead; that's got to mean I'm out now."

"Until Copland decides he wants you again. He must know what your haunted item is, right? He could come for you whenever he wants. Unless he thinks you're a liability. Two or three ghosts could track you down and tear you to shreds in minutes."

Kat shrugged, the threat meant nothing to her.

"So? I'm done with it, man. I don't care anymore."

Shane looked around the rooftop again. There had to be a fire escape somewhere. The west side of the building was close to its neighbor as well. He might be able to jump the alley between them.

"Do you care enough to want revenge?" Shane asked. The ghost stared at him with the eyeless pits in her skull.

"Revenge?"

"The simple kind," Shane said. "The end of Silvershore. Of Copland."

"You think you can kill him?" she asked.

"There's no one in the world who can't be killed," Shane pointed out.

"Just people who think they can't."

Kat made a face, and he couldn't read her expression. The eyeless gaze provided little insight into what the spirit was thinking. Finally, she pointed to the southwest corner of the building.

"You have to jump off the edge there. The roof of the next building drops just a little, but even you should be able to make it across."

"Even me," Shane said, looking at the corner of the roof.

"Make a run at it, though, or they'll scrape you out of the alley."

There was little time to ponder another course of action. Shane ran across the roof, the scorching sun overhead making sweat trickle down the small of his back even before the exertion of sprinting at an unknown jump.

The noise of the building's air conditioning masked the sound of his footfalls. Shane thought he heard the roof door open somewhere behind him, but there was no time to turn back and nothing to do even if he did. He reached the corner of the roof, took the small jump up to the ledge in his final stride, and then pushed off as hard as he could with his right leg.

For a moment that stretched like slow motion in his mind, Shane was weightless. He leaped across the chasm between buildings. The neighboring apartment was older and shorter, but only just. The roof was covered with lines of laundry hung out to dry, and a rooftop garden that someone had tended to grow vegetables. He could see it all coming toward him as he spanned the distance, his arms and legs extended as he descended.

He landed into a roll, the jolt of the fall rattling his teeth. His heart was in his throat, and his pulse raced as he pushed back to his feet with a grunt.

"South," Kat told him, already by his side. "This one's closer, should be easier."

Shane nodded and ran again, pushing past bleached white sheets and linens hanging from the multiple lines until he was in the clear. He built up a head of steam and leaped again, crossing a much narrower gap to a third building the same height as the one he left.

The new building, partially shaded by a taller one to the east, was home to many pigeons that had nested on the roof in various nooks and crannies. They cooed and ruffled their feathers at his arrival but otherwise ignored him. A ghost sat among them and watched Shane with silent curiosity.

"You can take a fire escape to the ground," Kat said as she pointed to the far corner of the building. "If you duck into the storm sewers, you can travel anywhere in the old city underground. The tunnels are big."

Shane looked back the way he had come. He could see some of the roof of Luther's building through the flapping sheets. Men were there, searching the area, but they had not seen his escape.

"Well, well, well. Little kitty trying to run away."

Kat cursed and Shane turned, hearing an unfamiliar voice speaking from behind him. Another ghost had appeared, one he recognized from Silvershore. The ghost that spent the night with the rooftop sniper at the company's office.

"Naughty, naughty," the ghost said, wagging his finger admonishingly in Kat's face.

"They found my—" Kat began. She blinked from existence before she could finish the sentence, leaving Shane alone with the new spirit.

"Her item," the ghost said, grinning at Shane. "That was what she was going to say. Popped her in a lead box, probably."

"Probably," Shane agreed.

The ghost was an average-looking man. He wore jeans and a T-shirt and seemed very unremarkable save for a waxy pallor to his skin and a faint haze over his eyes like he had cataracts. His accent was vaguely Texan.

"I heard you can kill ghosts," the spirit said. "But looking at you in person? You look like a freak, pal. Maybe you just scare everyone off."

"Maybe," Shane said, dropping his bag. If the police were with

Copland's men, then he had to assume they were also in Copland's pocket. That meant Shane's face would be known to every cop in Ravjek. Copland was hoping to bury Shane quickly.

The ghost opened his mouth to say something else, likely another random taunt. Shane's first hit was a punch to the ghost's nose, stunning him enough that he didn't even see Shane's leg kick out.

He took the ghost in the kneecap, causing him to collapse to all fours at Shane's feet. Pigeons fluttered and cooed as Shane stomped on the ghost's hand, and then grasped the ghost's head firmly.

Shane fell to his knees next to the spirit, forcing the ghost's head to the rooftop as he squeezed with all his might. The ghost cried out, grasping at his head, and trying to pull Shane's hands away even as his skull crumbled.

Pigeons burst into flight as the ghost exploded and knocked Shane back against the wall. Feathers fell like snow and Shane groaned, the force of the blast taking him square in the chest.

He lay on the ground for a beat, catching his breath, and trying not to think about the mess he was resting in. One of the cops had probably seen the great pigeon exodus. He had no time for rest.

Shane rolled to his side, picked himself up awkwardly, and retrieved his bag. He ran for the edge of the building, to the place Kat told him about, and found a rickety, rusted-out fire escape attached that led down to an alley below.

Metal creaked and groaned, shaking precariously as Shane climbed down. Bolts shuddered and pulled away from the wall, but he ignored them. Instead, he focused on taking the ladder down as swiftly as he could.

Once he was in the alley, Shane scanned the ground. His eyes fell on a storm grate near a series of garbage cans. It was piled with trash, but it was wide and hidden from plain view.

More sirens screamed through the city now. What might have started as a setup to have him detained was now a manhunt. The neighborhood would soon be overrun with police.

Shane pulled up the sewer grate, wincing at the smell that rose from the bowels of the city. But as Kat had pointed out, it was old and designed with large tunnels that could be easily traversed.

He dropped into the hole, pulling the grate down after him, and landed ankle-deep in sludge. The heat of the day made the tunnel humid and rancid. The smell was nearly overwhelming, not just waste but trash, stagnant water, and other rotten things. He was forced to pull the collar of his shirt over his face for some relief.

There were only two directions to travel. One led closer to Silvershore, still far on the other side of town.

That was the direction Shane took, leading him deep under the heart of the city, through its decayed and rotten guts.

CHAPTER 17
THE IRONWORKS

Shane traveled the tunnels beneath Ravjek for hours, surfacing briefly here and there to orient himself as the sludge-filled passages wound and meandered all over the city making it hard to stay on track toward any destination.

Every now and then he would pass another grate and hear the sounds of people talking, or traffic, and even more wailing sirens. He stayed in the shadows and made his way deeper into the city, closer to the industrial district Silvershore called home.

The tunnels only offered cover for so long. They had been built in a bygone era and were designed for the city when it was smaller. Whatever new system was built to accommodate the larger area didn't connect and soon Shane found himself at a dead end.

When he rose into another alley in a part of town he didn't recognize, the sun was at its hottest yet and the shade between buildings did little to stifle it.

Covered in filth, Shane slid the grate back in place and stayed crouched in the shadows as he observed his location. He was well past the downtown area, beyond his old hotel, the outdoor market, and Luther's apartment. Nothing looked familiar to him even though he had driven around the city to learn the lay of the land.

Cars passed the alley. The street had moderate traffic, but nothing like the core of the city. Foot traffic was brisk but not remarkable. It looked like he was perhaps at the edge of the industrial area he sought, maybe a couple of miles from Silvershore.

His clothes were caked in filth, and his smell must have been beyond overpowering. He looked suitably like some of the homeless he'd seen around the market and in the poorer parts of town, enough so that he suspected no one would pay him a second look out in the open.

Shane left the alley and crossed the street, heading down a second alley to a less-populated street one block over. He kept his head down and stayed in the shadows of buildings wherever possible, heading in the general direction he knew he needed to go.

Getting closer to Silvershore was a risk, but one he felt was worth taking. Copland expected him to make a move and would prepare appropriately. Shane just needed to stay a step ahead and do the unexpected.

Soon enough, Shane traveled down emptier streets, passing boarded-up buildings and empty lots overgrown with weeds. He was back on the industrial side of the city with its many abandoned factories.

Once he recognized his surroundings, Shane detoured from the path he was on and cut across a handful of properties, following old railroad tracks until he found the ironworks once more.

He could see Silvershore in the distance. He'd need to be cautious and stay out of sight until he was ready for them. To that end, Shane made his way into the abandoned ironworks.

The facility must have once employed hundreds of people. It was an enormous factory that covered a large swath of land. Tracks were fixed to steel support girders that held great chains and hooks and hoists. Once upon a time, they must have been used to lift large objects and transport them across the plant floor.

A series of huge blast furnaces lined the center of the building, each one equipped with a large vessel for smelting metal and wide beds that looked like primitive bathtubs, still crusted with ancient iron frozen in place where it had cooled and been forgotten.

After the plant closed, little was done to clean and strip down components. Nearly every inch of the building was covered with a sooty film, and spatters of black iron were on nearly every surface. Fragments of metal were all over the floors and machines.

Bins full of pig iron still lined the walls, outfitted with hooks for the roof chains to lift them and steel wheels to travel along train track-like paths in the floors.

For its size, the most noteworthy aspect of the plant was the lack of spirits. Nothing else in Ravjek was so devoid of ghosts, and for good reason. The amount of loose iron would have made it impossible for any ghost to safely navigate the building, at least for any length of time. It was like a minefield for the dead.

Shane walked the plant from end to end, on the ground, and along a catwalk overhead. He found an old office and break area at the building's farthest end, and racks and racks of old blue coveralls. He changed out of his rancid sewer clothes and into the darkest coveralls he could find, as well as a clean shirt that was partially moth-eaten but in relatively good condition otherwise.

Silvershore had suffered casualties, but it was hard to say how many, or how many mercs were still on the roster. There were enough, though. That was all that mattered. He would need to even the numbers and strike some fear into those that were left.

The day stretched on as Shane took stock of the supplies he'd gotten from Milos and what the ironworks facility afforded him. Literal tons of scrap iron were scattered around the building, ranging from bins of shavings to giant bars.

There were stacks of rebar and two bins of spaghetti-like braided steel wire that had been collected on giant spools, now partially unraveled. Other bins held heavier scrap, much of it too bulky and too rusted to be of much use. But some was salvageable.

Shane hadn't done any serious survival training in years, but he remembered it. He knew how to find food and water, he knew how to build a fire, and he knew how to set traps.

Day stretched into night. There were several entrances to the plant, and Shane used the braided wire and chains to rig all of them. Things needed to be fast and effective, not necessarily pretty.

Trip wires at each entrance connected to counterweighted rebar rigs that were lashed to sharpened iron spikes. They were crudely made but weighed more than a man, and when they fell, they'd swing with enough force to skewer anything within several feet of the door.

He set lines rigged to the overhead tracks and catwalks. Bins of shavings and scraps were balanced on the thinnest iron wedges, poised precariously over the few clear paths for humans or ghosts to travel.

As night fell, Shane slipped out of the rear of the building and made his way to the textile factory nearby, where he just walked in like he worked there.

Loud machines churned and spun yarn into fabric while employees sized, pulled, and cut lengths of the materials, and then sorted and finished edges among myriad other tasks.

Shane walked the floor with purpose, not making eye contact with anyone, until he found a supply room. He filled his bag with a handful of supplies he recognized—a few cleaners and common chemical compounds like hydrogen peroxide—then headed out again without speaking a word.

It was creeping into the early hours of the morning when Shane finished his work. He was forced to eyeball some measurements, and working in the sweltering heat made him a little nervous. The devices he'd put together were volatile, and easily triggered by heat or even friction. He was risking himself as much as he was risking damage to anyone who came for him if they went off at the wrong time.

The plant was ready, but Shane was not. He'd observed Silvershore before Reaper Company was after him, and now, he needed to see what had changed. He needed to know each man. Who they were, where they lived, and what they did with their time. He'd need to track them.

It took Shane an hour of walking the right kinds of streets in the wrong parts of town to find someone loitering around an alley who spoke English and was willing to take him to see someone else about making a deal. He ended up in the back room of a basement bar opposite a burly man named Vanko. Vanko smoked a large, unpleasant cigar and grinned at Shane from the moment he entered the room.

"I need a car," Shane said, reaching into his coveralls and pulling out the MCX-SPEAR rifle he'd taken off the fallen soldier in Kogar. He placed it on the desk in front of the other man.

"You... sell this?" Vanko asked. It took Shane a moment to realize Vanko's hesitation came from the fear that Shane had drawn the weapon to use it, not exchange it.

"You bet. Top of the line, latest U.S. military version of XM7," he said.

Vanko reached for it hesitantly and then gained confidence when Shane didn't make a move. He inspected the weapon, removed the partial clip, and nodded. For a criminal, he was an amiable man to deal with.

"What kind of car?" he asked, his Russian accent thick.

"Anything that won't get pulled over by the cops and won't break down in the next week."

"Anything?" Vanko asked.

"Anything," Shane repeated.

Vanko smiled and opened a drawer, rooting around for a moment before pulling out a keychain.

"Out back. Ugly brown Citroën. Belongs to my cousin Klaus. He's in prison for six more years; he won't miss it."

"Pleasure doing business with you," Shane said, taking the keys.

"American," Vanko said, stopping him at the door. "I see your picture, you know. People are looking for you."

"I know," Shane said, his hand squeezing into a fist around the keys.

"Not a problem, is it?"

"Not for me," Vanko said. "Sounds like trouble for you, maybe. You take car and leave town?"

"No," Shane said. "I'm taking the car and killing everyone who's after me."

Vanko laughed around his cigar and Shane left the building, heading to a small parking lot behind the bar. There were only three cars there. The Citroën was halfway under an old tarp and was ugly but forgettable. The front end was made with some odd angles and seemed weirdly boxy, but it would fit in around town and fade into a crowd well.

Now, it's time to hunt, Shane thought.

He returned to the factory, ready to set a plan into motion.

CHAPTER 18

ON THE HUNT

Shane had been living out of the ironworks for four days. He had used this time to gather intel on the members of Silvershore, following their comings and goings with every spare hour he had. He had followed every soldier to their home, including Copland. He had tracked their movements in their downtime, from where they went to what they ate and when they traveled to and from the office.

He was spreading himself thin, tracking all the soldiers, and it left him unable to focus wholly on anyone to learn their full routines, but it didn't matter. He just needed the basics. The men did very little that was out of character in the time he spent observing any of them.

None of the soldiers had family in the country, so most of them just went home to eat, sleep, and maybe work out. Their work at Silvershore took up most of their time.

The easiest target that Shane identified to start was a corporal named Preston Simms. Every day so far, Simms went home and then ran for thirty minutes before returning home.

Shane followed Simms from Silvershore to his apartment. He waited until the mercenary headed out for his afternoon run and then drove to the rear of the building, parked, and made his way inside.

The board in the lobby said Simms lived on the third floor. Shane made his way up the stairs to the apartment and tried the knob. He'd left it unlocked.

Shane entered the apartment, which was decorated much more lavishly than Luther's. Simms was a sports fan and had various posters on his walls and themed decorations in the kitchen, which waited on the other side of the door as Shane entered.

"You forget something?" a voice asked.

Shane closed the door as Simms' partner, an older spirit with a bald head and a huge scar across his neck, came out of an adjacent room.

"No," Shane answered simply.

The ghost rushed him without another word. They met in the kitchen, and Shane drove his elbow into the ghost's neck, forcing it against the wall. He kneed the spirit in the groin and pulled it to the ground before rolling him onto his stomach.

"You're a dead man," the ghost growled as Shane planted his knee in the small of the ghost's back.

"Sorry, not a lot of time to chat today," he replied. He reached under the ghost's head, grabbed his chin, and then wrenched his head violently to the side. The ghost's neck broke with a muffled crunch. Shane kept turning, and with his knee holding firm in the ghost's back, he pushed up at the same time.

The head detached from the ghost's body. Everything expanded violently, and the blast of energy flowed in all directions. Shane fell to the ground and sat there for a moment, catching his breath.

He repositioned himself, out of sight just beyond the door, and waited for Simms to return. The corporal was back right on schedule, entering the apartment and kicking off his shoes while breathing heavily.

"It's hotter today than it was yesterday," he yelled into the apartment, half laughing. He wore shorts and a T-shirt, leaving him unarmed and unprepared. As soon as he closed the door, Shane slammed into him.

"Don't forget to hydrate," he said, taking a handful of Simms' hair in his hand and holding it tightly as he knocked the man's face into the wall.

Simms groaned and Shane quickly bound his wrists with zip ties before throwing him to the floor.

"If you're wondering about your partner, don't. He didn't last five minutes, and he won't be coming back. You can join him, or you can tell me what I need to know."

"I don't know anything," Simms growled. Shane knelt beside the man and took him by the hair once more, bouncing his face quickly off the floor as he looked around the apartment. The kitchen dead ahead had been tidy until the ghost exploded, knocking things aside. To the right and down a short hall was the living room, featuring a handful of posters and a basketball hoop fixed above another doorway.

"Nice place you have here. How long do you think you'd survive if I lit it on fire?"

"I don't know anything," Simms repeated. "I'm not in charge of anything."

Shane smashed the man's head again.

"You should probably wait until I ask a question before pretending to not know the answer."

Simms groaned and spit blood on the floor.

"Then what? What do you need to know?"

"Is Copland working for Janosik?" Shane asked.

"What?"

He slammed Simms' head again.

"Not an answer. Is Copland working for Janosik?"

"Man, I don't—"

Another bounce off the floor, and he cried out in pain. There was a growing pool of blood under his face.

"Is Copland working for Janosik?"

"I don't know!" Simms yelled. "I don't know the client. None of us do."

"Was killing Blakely part of the job?"

"Yes. He and Leclerc and Washington. And you," Simms admitted.

"Because…"

"The hell do you mean?"

Another bounce and Shane heard a muffled crunch as Simms' nose broke.

"You're going against the Reapers, man! Blakely sold us out to the enemy, so he had to go. You're working for the wrong side, you get burned. That's it. That's how it goes."

"I'm not working for anyone," Shane pointed out. "Your boss murdered Blakely to take over the company, and you didn't even question it?"

"He went to meet with the target and got shot. We didn't have anything to do with it."

"Copland shot him," Shane corrected. "Then he took control of the company, and you guys turned on Luther Washington. Stunning work, soldier."

"You'll say anything to save your ass," Simms muttered. Shane laughed and leaned closer to him.

"If you haven't noticed, you're the one tied up and bleeding. I don't need to be saved."

"You will," the corporal said.

"And what do you think *you're* going to need after Copland finds out you talked to me?"

Simms scoffed, struggling in his bonds.

"I didn't tell you anything."

"I'm sure Copland will believe you, too. I'm going to let you live, Preston. That way Copland can wonder why you survived when no one else has. Not like the man has a track record of killing his guys, right?"

"It's not going to work. I'll tell him you're setting me up."

"Sure," Shane said. "What did Luther say before he died? Or Leclerc? Bet they had lots of reasons not to be murdered that no one listened to."

Simms was breathing more heavily and struggling against his bonds.

"You can't do this. I didn't do anything!"

"Tell me what job Copland has you working on here."

"It's political. It's rebels, man. Terrorists. We've been hitting these camps, looking for this guy Zemba, the one who took out Blakely. The guy they said took out Blakely. He's leading the faction against the President."

"Who lives in these camps?" Shane asked.

"What?"

He smashed Simms' face off the floor again and the man cried out, clenching his teeth to muffle it.

"Who?" Shane asked.

"Terrorists! I told you!"

"You've seen them? The terrorists in the camps?"

"We get the intel, and we go. Long-range stuff. We don't go in and engage; we'd be outnumbered."

"So, you could be killing anyone. Civilians. Families. You have no idea."

"It's good intel," Simms countered. Shane wondered if the people who bombed Kogar had good intel, too. Hell, it might have come from the same source.

"Who gives you the intel, Simms?" Shane asked quietly, leaning down close to the man.

"What?"

Another bounce off the floor, and the blood splattered with a slapping sound. Simms nearly sobbed as he bit back another scream.

"Goddammit. It's from a source. It's from a spy in the group who works for—"

"Says who? Think about what the hell I'm asking you," Shane interrupted. Simms struggled a moment trying to understand the question.

"What do you want me to say? It's Copland. The CO always gives us orders, briefs us on missions. Did you make up your missions when you were a Marine or something?"

"My orders never included killing my friends," Shane told him. "And if they did, I sure would be suspicious about the people they were telling me were my enemies if I never saw them in person. Any of these terrorists ever take a shot at you? Ever catch them on your scope building bombs? Torturing civilians? Anything?"

"You're crazy, man. Blakely turned on us. He was working for the enemy. Leclerc and Washington, too."

"Is that why Luther was running for Budapest instead of the terrorists he worked for? Is that why an entire town full of ghosts watched Blakely's partner stab him in the heart in front of Copland and then drag him out of Kogar for you guys to bring home?"

"How do you know he died in Kogar?"

"The dead there told me, Simms. Told me it was a setup. Blakely thought he could negotiate peace and not have to kill anyone, but Copland was waiting for him. There was no meet with any terrorist. There are no terrorists. Silvershore was bought by the Vakovians to squash political dissent and ensure the President stays in office. You guys are hired hitmen, bolstering the party line. You're a propaganda tool."

"You don't know what you're talking about," Simms spat, struggling against Shane.

"You murdered three Marines for money. You're closer to a terrorist than Blakely ever was."

"I didn't pull the trigger," Simms shouted. "I wasn't even there when Blakely died. I didn't pop Luther. You can't lay this on me."

"No? You're still getting paid, aren't you? Sounds like you're as much to blame as anyone."

Shane pressed the edge of the iron knuckles against the back of Simms' head. Face down, bleeding, and already in a panic, it would have felt about the right size and hardness to be a gun barrel.

"Please! Come on, man! I didn't kill anyone," Simms begged.

"Did Luther beg?" Shane asked.

"It's not what you think, okay? Blakely didn't think he was meeting any politician or terrorist. He thought he was meeting a journalist. That's what got him killed. He was going to sell us out!"

Shane exhaled loudly, staring at the back of Simms' head, his brow knit in confusion.

"What are you talking about?"

"It was all just a job, like you said. The Vakovians wanted to paint these people as monsters, that was all. We were supposed to go liquidate their camps. Foreign contractors who were fired upon by political dissidents. The government's hands are clean, we're not involved officially, and no one looks bad except the dead guys," Simms explained, his words running out so fast he was nearly babbling. Shane pressed the metal harder against the soldier's skull.

"And?"

"And Blakely found out the truth and refused to take the contract. He was going to talk to some British reporter, expose the Vakovians, but it was Copland, playing him. They set a meet, and next time I saw Blakely, he was dead."

"What about Washington and Leclerc?" Shane asked.

"Liabilities, man! Copland already took the job. We'd wiped out an entire camp, and it was families. Just displaced families and people against the President's policies."

"You killed them?"

"I didn't know! None of us knew at the time. After, Copland said we were all-in, that we were washed in the same blood. He took me aside privately and told me now that he knew he could trust me, maybe we could do something about my mom back home. She's sick; she's got a lot of bills. He said he takes care of his friends. But if he couldn't trust me, there's no telling what could happen to her. He was threatening my family, man!"

Shane slammed the soldier's head against the ground one last time and put the iron knuckles back in his pocket. Copland was piling lies on lies. Blakely was meeting a terrorist. He was meeting a reporter. He was lying to everyone.

"You killed families, Simms," he pointed out. "You put your ass and your bank account above Blakely and Washington and all those people you 'liquidated'."

Shane stood, looking down at the blood splattered across the floor. Part of him wanted to kill Simms, but there was no point. He had the information he needed. There was no way he'd out himself for committing what amounted to war crimes to cover for anything else. The details were not significantly different from what Shane already knew.

Copland killed Blakely for not getting with the program. The program just happened to be killing civilians to keep the government of Vakovia in power. Lives for cash, monsters for hire.

"They'd kill me if I didn't go along, and you know it. I'd be lined up with Blakely and Washington right now. Call me a coward if you want, but I didn't come to this goddamn country to die," Simms said.

"What did you come here for, soldier?" Shane asked.

Simms was face-down in blood, straining to breathe through his broken nose. He faced the wall, away from Shane, and grunted.

"This Friday," Simms said, his voice flat. "Zemba's supposed to be coming to Ravjek for an interview ahead of the next election. It's all supposed to go down before he gets there."

"Where?" Shane asked.

"Don't know yet. Only Copland does."

Shane made his way to the apartment door.

"Get out of the country, Simms," he said. Simms laughed bitterly.

"They'll find me. You should just kill me now," he said.

"Nah," Shane replied. "You're not worth it."

He left the apartment and closed the door behind him.

CHAPTER 19

KICKING THE HIVE

"You kill a lot of people," Vanko said around one of his smelly cigars.

"Hmm?"

"You're wanted. Again. Deaths of two American soldiers," the Russian replied. He pushed aside some things on his desk and pulled out a newspaper. "Luther Washington and Preston Simms."

Vanko turned the paper and showed it to Shane.

Copland doesn't care about losing men if it means covering his tracks and pinning it all on me.

After Shane left Simms' apartment, he returned to the ironworks. He left early the next morning to get some more supplies. Vanko had offered him coffee and cigarettes, and it had been days since he'd had either, so he accepted. The Russian had proven to be a reliable contact.

Shane exhaled a lungful of smoke and shrugged. The Ravjek police had pinned the deaths of every fallen Reaper Company member on him. Everyone lost in Kogar, Washington, Leclerc, Simms... everyone but Blakely. His death still needed to be blamed on Zemba.

By local understanding, Shane was now a serial killer. That was at least ten murders. He almost didn't want to know what the police were saying about him.

"Simms was shot?" Shane asked.

"Did you not shoot him?" Vanko asked back.

Shane raised an eyebrow, and the Russian laughed deeply. He rustled the paper again.

"Let us see. Hmm. Preston Simms was found shot in his apartment," he said. "Yes, you shot him."

It amused Vanko no end that Shane was an American being set up by other Americans. Shane was fairly certain that was part of the reason the man was willing to help him. He enjoyed watching the story unfold even though he was as aware as Shane was that the police were in Copland's pocket. The Ravjek police were, according to Vanko, easier to buy than a loaf of bread.

"They are talking about calling in the military for you," Vanko added.

"The military? Why? According to who?"

"Police chief. You are a public menace. A danger to innocent civilians, and police are overwhelmed."

"Seriously?"

Vanko shrugged.

"More or less. If military comes for you, it will be ugly."

Shane could only assume Vanko was correct. None of it sounded reasonable, and none of it was. He wondered if Copland had signed off on the idea. It sounded like unwanted attention to Shane, the kind that might get international notice if he wasn't careful. This was partially why Blakely was killed, if Simms was to be believed.

Maybe the Ravjek police would inadvertently ruin Copland's work in Vakovia. Of course, Shane would still end up dead if that was how everything played out. He needed to get Copland put away before things escalated.

A knock came at the door of Vanko's office.

"Come in," the Russian said.

One of his men entered carrying two packages. Shane put out his cigarette and stood, but the man handed them to Vanko, who then passed them to Shane.

"You sell me gun and then come for body armor. You have things backward, friend," the Russian said as Shane inspected what he'd been given. He needed something powerful enough to withstand shots from a sniper rifle if it came to that.

"We'll see," Shane said, tossing Vanko an envelope of cash, most of what he had left. One way or another, his time in Vakovia was coming to an end.

"You want umbrella? Weather calls for rain today, break in this heatwave," the Russian said, nodding to a pair of them hanging from a coat rack by the door.

"No need to hide from the rain," Shane said. The other man shrugged.

"I hope you survive," he said as Shane made his way to the door.

"That's what this is for," Shane replied, holding up the second package. Vanko's laughter followed him out.

Inside the ironworks, Shane had set up a perch on the catwalk inside the plant to spy on Silvershore. He used tin snips to cut through the exterior wall, giving him a hole big enough to use binoculars to monitor the building while remaining out of sight.

After his visit with Simms, the routine had changed. They must have realized Shane had tracked Simms' movements, and that was how he found him so soon after he returned home the previous day.

Now, everyone's schedule was shaken up. None of them came and went as they had before, and it looked like everyone planned to hunker down in the office as the end of the day came with no one leaving.

Whatever work Shane had done in tracking the others to their homes was now useless. Plus, if the military was being called in for whatever stupid reason, Shane's window for action was closing.

The ironworks was as fortified as he could make it. There was no reason to draw things out any longer. He would make his move on Copland and lure the unit into his traps.

He waited for nightfall, observing Silvershore while staying out of sight. When it was dark enough, he made his way to the floor. He changed into darker clothes and the vest he had purchased from Vanko.

The Russian had told him that the weather called for rain, and there were already rumblings of thunder as the clouds began to build in the dark sky, concealing the moon and the stars.

Copland would have planned for a lot of scenarios. No doubt the guards and their routines had been shaken up inside Silvershore's HQ, and they probably had some traps of their own. Trying his luck wouldn't be worth it. They were expecting him.

Shane needed to throw everyone off their game. Copland might keep a cool head, but he couldn't stop everyone else from getting rattled and making mistakes. Especially if they were properly provoked. That was why Shane had spent the bulk of his money on the second package.

Shane carried the case from the dark plant door to the edge of the fence that led to the ironworks parking lot. He knelt next to the weeds and shrubs that grew there and opened it. He was about three hundred feet from the exterior of the building and would be spotted soon, if he hadn't been already.

The RPG-7 only weighed about twenty pounds. It was remarkably affordable as well. Vanko had good suppliers.

Shane loaded the Bulgarian rocket into the launch tube and lifted the RPG to his shoulder, adjusting his sights to Copland's office window. It was a terrible choice to have an office at the front of the building. He pulled the trigger.

The rocket burst from the tube trailing fire and smoke. Shane tossed the launcher and ran back to the ironworks without waiting to confirm his hit. There were no second chances and no time to revel in a clean shot or lament a bad one. He had given himself away.

The explosion shook the ground and sent a bright burst of flame into the night that briefly illuminated the ironworks and everything around it. Shane looked back as he ran, laughing despite himself, as the second floor of Silvershore's office collapsed onto what had once been Copland's office.

There was no way to know if he'd been lucky enough to take Copland out with the strike, but even if he hadn't, he had definitely ruffled some feathers.

Men yelled at each other in the night, and someone fired a weapon. Shane didn't even hear the bullet and wasn't sure if it was shot in his direction or just a blind attempt to hit anything.

He made it back to the plant, sidestepped his trip wires, and then ducked under a series of randomly hung iron chains, pausing in the door to look back. Silvershore was burning, the rocket had hit something significant, and the fire was consuming the building. He could see figures silhouetted against the flames, including a trio making its way toward his location with weapons drawn.

Two ghosts flanked the approaching soldiers. Shane could not see the third but knew there had to be one out there somewhere, and more would come to reinforce them. He fell back into the plant, making his way to one of the large bins of pig iron to take cover.

There was a stillness in the plant, with the walls cutting off the sounds of the fire at Silvershore and the ambient noise of the city at night. The place just had a sense of emptiness inside, made to feel that much larger by the sound of the old blast furnace humming in the middle of the building.

Lightning filled the sky overhead, flashing through the openings in the roof where ceiling panels had rusted or peeled away. Thunder boomed and shook the building,

Shane spread soot from the floor across his face and receded into the shadows. On the far side of the plant, he watched a ghost pass through an exit door he'd left open and vanish soundlessly as it stepped across a minefield of scattered iron filings.

At the nearest door, the one he'd passed through only moments earlier, the first of the three Silvershore soldiers arrived alongside his spectral asset. Shane could not see the other two from where he'd taken cover, but he assumed they had taken up defensive positions.

The ghosts headed in first. One hit the chains hanging above the door like a cheap seventies-era beaded curtain and was forced back. The other was smart enough to duck low and sidestep some of the iron on the floor.

Shane recognized the spirit from his earlier reconnaissance, a middle-aged man whose scalp had been pulled from his head. The ghost proceeded deeper into the ironworks, but Shane kept his eyes on the door and the soldier there. He moved slowly, but he was progressing, following the spirit's lead.

The soldier bent low to avoid jostling the chains. His attention was on them and not on his feet. He stepped on one of the nearly invisible filament lines Shane had stretched across the door.

The line pulled and released a pipe bomb fixed to the door frame. It hit the ground with a metallic clink and the chemical reaction inside took over.

The homemade device exploded violently, rocking the facility. Shane covered his head and ducked as the device shook the bomb on the other side of the door and set it off as well, doubling the size of the blast.

Fire and iron scattered in all directions, and despite the danger, Shane had to stifle a panicked laugh. He had eyeballed the ingredients when he put the devices together and was afraid he hadn't made them powerful enough or stable enough. They were definitely not stable, but they had proved more than powerful.

Parts of the exterior walls collapsed, with fire burning in small piles across the entrance to the ironworks and even several yards past the door, where shrapnel and debris had been thrown. There was no sign of the soldier, but Shane had inadvertently ensured the others had a clear entrance to the building, now that the rest of his doorway traps had been destroyed. He had hoped to catch at least one more with the second device, but that would not be the case.

The distraction of the blast opened the floor for Shane to move, using smoke and flame as cover. He dashed from the hiding place next to the pig iron across the production floor to the blast furnace.

Heat rose in waves from the base of the tall, bottle-shaped structure the size of a house. He had spent the early part of the day rewiring the facility and getting power back. That allowed him to start the blast furnace and get it slowly up to the proper temperature. He had just short of no idea how to use the machine, but he hoped his general idea was enough.

More lightning shot through the darkness, and another boom of thunder shook the building's unsteady walls. The rain would come soon.

Belts whirred to life as he hit the red button on a control panel. Pig iron chunks were carried up to the building's upper level and dumped in the opening to the blast furnace.

As the iron began to melt, Shane flipped a series of switches. The metal hoppers that hung from chains came to life with a pained, metallic grinding sound as the old, dry metal gears squealed and lurched. They moved along the metal track, swaying and groaning, as other machines, including smaller furnaces, churned and rumbled to life.

The already-hot facility was becoming scorching, and Shane could see the blazing, red glow at the base of the furnace getting brighter and whiter. He ducked next to the control panel and watched the door as the smoke and fire died down, waiting to see what the Reapers had next.

"Looking for someone?"

The ghost that had entered the ironworks fell on him from behind. He wrapped his hands around Shane's neck, nails piercing the flesh like the blades of chisels.

"Isn't it about time you were dead?"

CHAPTER 20
TIME TO DIE

Shane's elbow shot back into the ghost's groin. A second elbow on the other side hit the spirit in the side of his knee. The icy hands slipped from Shane's neck, and he watched as the ghost fell back onto a splatter of old, melted iron before vanishing.

Sparks exploded off the control panel as a bullet hit the metal case a few inches to Shane's left. He ducked low as a second bullet zipped past and hit the blast furnace behind him. More shots rang out, a blanket fire now, spraying haphazardly across the plant.

Shane crawled across the floor to the catwalk stairs, looking for the shooter. Beneath the stairs, he had a partially obscured view of the ghost that had just vanished. It stood next to a pile of twisted metal that fell when the explosives went off. The shooter was well-covered but also inside the walls of the plant.

Above the shooter and the ghost, braided steel line was still fixed to the beams and had not been dislodged by the explosion. Shane followed the line with his eyes and scrambled to the far side of the stairs where he'd tied it down earlier, to pull it free.

The shooter got off one last shot, barely missing Shane as he loosened the cable. A mesh of rebar spikes swung down from the catwalk above. Shane guessed he'd made them with about two hundred pounds of metal, but it was hard to say. Enough to make sure whoever was below would feel it.

The shooter didn't make a sound. Rebar tore through his cover and slammed with a dull thump into the man's body. The ghost was briefly displaced as well, but his haunted item had to be on the shooter's person. The spirit returned in a blink, just a few feet from where he'd vanished.

Someone shouted at the far door where the first ghost had disappeared. The door pulled open, and the spirit next to the now-dead shooter looked up.

"Watch the door. Watch the door!" the ghost yelled.

One of the Reapers stepped inside, unable to hear the ghost over the sounds of the furnace. The second trip line went off, and another explosion tore a hole in the building's side. A third explosion ripped open the far end just a second later, and the final device went off. Fire and debris rained down as shouts rang out over the sounds of machinery.

Something spattered on Shane's face, and he looked up. A drop of rain had made its way through the patchy roof. The storm was beginning.

Ghosts filtered in from all sides. Shane counted eight spirits from his vantage point. The heat of the plant was growing to dangerous levels. Molten iron was already running from the blast furnace and down a channel, to where it was meant to be collected. After years of neglect and no one around to ensure the facility was running properly, the glowing metal was overflowing along its path and spilling out onto the ground.

Sparks exploded as the molten metal consumed everything in its path. Smoke filled the building and obscured views, stinging Shane's eyes, and making it harder to breathe.

Raindrops fell into the glowing mass, hissing and sending steam into the air. The rain picked up its pace, and soon, steam was mixing with smoke to create a blinding haze. The noise of the facility was nearly deafening, a constant rumbling and droning that swallowed everything else.

Blue lightning crackled across the sky, and the peal of thunder that followed was ear-splitting. Then, the sky opened, and rain fell in a deluge. The partial roof could only hold back so much.

Steam hissed as the water pelted the blast furnace, already up to temperatures well over one thousand degrees Celsius. The smoke and steam rolled like the storm clouds above as Shane darted toward the pig iron bins.

The nearest ghost was pacing carefully between piles of iron bits on the floor. Shane grabbed the ghost from behind, kicking out a knee, and falling back with him to the ground. He didn't even see the ghost's face to identify which one it might have been.

With hands clutching the ghost's skull tightly, Shane twisted as they fell so the ghost landed face-first. The momentum and his body weight were all Shane needed to cause the ghost flesh to buckle under the pressure.

The ghost's head exploded the moment it hit the ground. The sound was swallowed by the roar of the furnace and the raging steam jets. Shane was cast aside like a rag doll and landed under an open ceiling panel. Cold, fat droplets of rain pelted him in the face, and he reveled in it for as long as he dared before getting back to his feet.

A great gout of molten metal erupted from one of the hoppers as a ceiling panel collapsed in the rain and dumped gallons of water into it. Someone let out a shrill and powerful cry of agony as flesh was consumed by white-hot iron.

Ghosts popped in and out of view as they fell prey to the stray iron and were launched back to their haunted items again and again. A pair of snare wires were tripped, dragging two mercenaries into the air by their ankles. A gunshot rang out and hit one of the ensnared men in the head before the other screamed and waved his hands, trying to warn the shooter from taking another shot.

Itchy trigger fingers, Shane thought. Through the smoke and steam, they were shooting at anything that moved.

"Ryan!" a voice shouted, nearly swallowed by the cacophony. Shane stayed out of sight, silent and unmoving as his name was called out again.

"You think you'll survive this? I will bring this place down on your head!"

Copland, in full tactical gear like his men, stood at a safe distance from the blast furnace. His skeletal partner was at his side, hunched over, and looking as angry as ever. Shane focused on Copland. He was not close enough to any of the remaining traps. But he was getting awfully close to the molten iron.

"Vox here wants me to let him gut you. I've seen him do it," Copland continued. Shane stayed still. Whatever the man was trying to provoke, it wasn't working very well. He wasn't sure what Copland was trying to prove other than maybe to waste time, but that was to his detriment as much as Shane's. The longer he and his men stayed in the plant, the more they risked their lives.

As if in answer to Shane's question, one of the mercenaries ran up behind Copland and handed him a tablet. The two talked though Shane couldn't make out what was said.

"Nashua, New Hampshire," Copland yelled. "One-two-five Berkley Street. Looks like... well, looks like a dump, to be honest."

He turned the tablet around and flashed the image on the screen. Shane could not make it out through the haze, but knew Copland wasn't pretending. He knew where Shane lived.

"Do you live alone, Ryan? Our recon says you do not. Says there's at least one ghost in there who likes to stare out of your windows like a dog waiting for its master. Who might that be?"

Shane looked to the catwalk. He might be able to get above Copland, especially if he kept talking. If he could jump down from behind, he could knock him into the spilling piles of molten iron. The ghost, Vox, would still be an issue to contend with, but the iron would keep him from acting too freely. Might. Maybe. Could. It was all a risk.

"James Moran. Is that a ghost?" Copland yelled. He scrolled through the tablet. "No, he's alive. A friend? What about... Francis Benedict? Uh... Victor Daniels? Jacinta Perez?"

Shane grunted. Their intel was old. What were they using? They had not been to his home recently. Jacinta's name should not have been on anyone's list if they were using up-to-date files. Copland was swinging for the fences.

Unless he wasn't, Shane thought. He cursed himself as Copland lowered the tablet and another man came to him, handing him what looked like a heavy black belt cluttered with small objects.

"You've been a real pain in the ass, Ryan. I hope you burn," the colonel yelled. He pulled something off the belt and then threw the thing toward the center of the room before turning and running for the exit.

Shane watched the thrown object, trying to focus on it through the haze. The rain battered his face and the smoke obscured his line of sight, but he could see the object spinning end over end through the plant toward the furnace. A tactical belt strapped with at least a dozen grenades. Copland had pulled the pin from one.

Lightning lit the sky again, and Shane crouched behind a bin of pig iron. They were heavy steel and had to weigh at least a couple of tons. He braced himself as thunder and grenades went off as one.

The sound was like hell had opened. Shane clapped his hands over his ears. The earth shook beneath him, and hot air seared across his face. The walls buckled, already damaged from his homemade explosives, and were blown outward.

The catwalk groaned and rolled over on itself, crashing to the ground in pieces. Fire spread in all directions while the immense blast furnace shook and began to tumble over.

The top of the furnace was at least sixty feet up, and it crumpled against the belts that fed it iron chunks. The belt system collapsed as the metal bent under the stress of the falling furnace tower.

Panels from the ceiling fell to the ground, splashing water as they went, creating more steam and more explosive blasts as molten metal spilled out uncontrollably from the furnace's base.

A handful of additional screams tore through the building as more of Copland's men, not privy to their commander's plan, fell victim to the searing heat or falling debris.

The base of the furnace groaned loudly, and Shane scrambled to his feet as the tower fell. Steel girders and supports snapped like twigs, and the building shuddered as the furnace toppled, dragging everything down with it.

Smoke and steam rose into the night in great clouds, mingling with the downpour outside. The hissing of the furnace's interior, now fully exposed to the rain, blocked out all other sounds.

The steam cloud rolled like a fog. Shane ran with it, crossing the collapsed wall into the parking lot next to the building.

When the furnace hit the ground, the tower cracked open like an egg. Molten metal crackled and sputtered in the rain. The few support beams left standing swayed and then toppled as well.

Shane made his way across the side parking lot to the trees and overgrowth of weeds. The scream of sirens was already filling the night as he escaped the raging noise of the ironworks' interior.

Flashing lights were parked across the street as fire crews worked to put out the blaze at Silvershore. More were approaching the ironworks alongside police cruisers.

In the glare of the assembled headlights, Shane could see Copland standing near the parking lot's entrance. Police ignored him and the other Reaper Company soldiers, despite them all being openly armed, and filled in the parking lot at a safe distance.

Only three men converged on Copland, while ghosts milled about in the shadows beyond. Shane waited and watched, and no more showed up. Three were left; the rest must have found their end in the plant.

Shane watched as one of the ghosts vanished, pulled away unexpectedly in the middle of a conversation. The others were pushed back as though an unexpected downburst of air came from the storm.

Shane realized after a moment it was the blast from the spirit. Inside the plant, another small explosion sent red hot metal into the air. A haunted item had been consumed by fire and destroyed, taking the ghost along with it.

The other spirits were sent into a panic. Those whose items were still on the bodies of the dead mercenaries in the plant were at risk of destruction, and they knew it.

Vox stood away from the others, uninterested in their concerns, and instead focused on what Copland was saying to the three remaining men. Another ghost was with them, and Shane's eyes narrowed. He recognized the burned face from the diner back in Nashua. It was Blakely's partner, the one who had betrayed him. The one who had killed him. Now Shane just needed to find a way to get to him.

CHAPTER 21
NATURE'S FURY

Clouds billowed up from the ironworks as the last of the molten metal was exposed to the open air and rain. Firefighters pulled back, forcing the police to retreat with them, and eventually, Copland and his small number of men.

The smell in the air was enough to let Shane know the problem. He could feel it in his lungs, acrid and bitter, and it made his eyes water. Whatever toxic fumes were being released as the plant melted down to slag were as deadly as the flames and unstable structure. The event was probably an ecological disaster for the area, and the rain washing away the metals and chemicals would pollute the land as much as the smoke polluted the air. It had not been his intention, but there was nothing to be done for it now.

His more immediate concern was staying alive. That and ensuring the opposite for Copland. The man must have had horseshoes up his backside to have survived the RPG strike on Silvershore and the chaos of the ironworks. His stubborn refusal to die grated on Shane's nerves.

If Shane let Copland escape, he was not sure how or where he'd get another chance at the man. But with so many police around, not to mention the ghosts and Copland's soldiers, there didn't seem to be any way to reach him. Not at that moment, anyway. The window had closed, and he needed to accept it.

The mission was a partial success. Silvershore was crippled, reduced to a handful of soldiers. Their headquarters was a smoldering ruin. They could still potentially go ahead with their mission to take out Zemba, but

Copland would need to pull it off with such a reduced team and resources. The problem was, Silvershore had the capability to do that. All he needed to do was locate Zemba and let Vox and the other ghosts do the rest. Shane might have prevented nothing.

He wanted to curse out loud. He wanted to rush across the parking lot and slam Copland's head with a chunk of pig iron before taking the ghost of Blakely's partner and pulling his head from his shoulders. But none of that was practical or helpful. Nothing would ever be so easy.

Shane crept through the weeds around to the rear of the lot. He moved slowly and deliberately, using the weather and the noise to shield himself from the living and the dead. It was not in his nature to retreat from a fight before it was finished, but this was not a battle he would win. This was not a retreat but a regrouping.

He had expected to have to flee if things didn't go as planned. His escape plan was not detailed or elaborate. Instead, it was simply a sewer grate he'd rigged for easy opening and sealing afterward to make it look like it was untouched. Ravjek had horrible sewers, but they were easily traversed and offered an unseen escape. It was better than dying.

Ghosts were patrolling the outskirts of the ironworks, unable to enter the chaos but still searching the exterior. It was hard to tell if they were searching for Shane or for their dead human counterparts. Shane avoided them, keeping low in the weeds and waiting for them to pass.

It was not clear if the ones who had lost their living partners would continue to serve in Reaper Company. Any ghost could have loyalties to a single person, but to the group as a whole? The dead were often fickle. Until he had evidence otherwise, Shane would have to assume they were still fighting for Copland.

When there were no spirits in sight, Shane made his way to the thick grate that covered the sewer at the far end of the parking lot. It had once been designed to handle runoff from the plant, and the entrance was wide enough for two men to enter. It was heavy and had been partially rusted in place, but some work with a pry bar had loosened it up and made it a viable passageway.

With one last look around to make sure he was not being observed, Shane opened the grate and dropped down under the parking lot. The rains had loosened a lot of muck, and the drop was a shorter but wetter one this time around. He landed with a splash that splattered his face and cursed quietly as he wiped himself clean.

So, what's the plan? If Shane's window for taking out Blakely's partner and Copland was closing, he needed a quick pivot. They needed to stay in the city to finish their mission to take out Zemba, but they would not be anywhere Shane had already seen them. What did that mean? What could Shane exploit in that situation?

He had mapped the sewer for a short distance in two directions. He headed east, away from Silvershore and the center of the city. The tunnels were dark, but he didn't risk using a light so close to where Copland and his team were. Instead, he let his hand guide him, keeping steady and ignoring what he might touch as he went.

The rain had thrown an unexpected kink into his plans. His trial runs in the sewer had been during the dry heatwave, and they were full of nothing but ankle-deep, rancid pools. Now, the water flowed freely and rapidly up to his shins as he trudged awkwardly forward. The smell had improved drastically, but it was the only real benefit of working his way through the rainstorm.

Copland was a hunter, and that was something Shane thought he could use. The distraction in the ironworks with the tablet and showing Shane he knew where he lived and who his friends were was a taunt. As skilled as Copland might be, and as long as he had been a soldier, he was still easily provoked. He couldn't let someone else win. His ego would not let Shane get away. He'd need proof of Shane's death, or he would not give up.

The water pushed Shane from behind, but with his hand on the wall, he could stay steady enough that it wasn't a danger. It was still shallow enough that even if he slipped on some unseen filth, he was not at great risk of being swept away. Not yet anyway.

The sound in the sewer was like being inside of a waterfall. It reminded Shane of the raging torrent he could hear but not see in Kogar, only now he was in the middle of it.

He trudged onward. The rain continued unabated in the world above, making the flow and the ever-growing roar increase moment after moment in the world below.

Shane had mapped a fair amount of sewer tunnels in his preparations for taking on Silvershore, but the storm was making it impractical. He would need to cut his journey short and return to the surface sooner than he planned once he was a safe distance from the plant and could slip away unseen. If the rain didn't relent, the tunnels would kill him.

Water that had just been at his shins now rushed about his knees, making it increasingly hard to move. If Shane left too soon, though, he'd end up in the sights of the police or maybe even some of the spirits. He needed more distance.

Progress was slow, and he cursed the rains again. His escape plan called for speed and stealth, and having just one of those was not doing him a lot of favors.

Shane went over the path in his head. He had planned to reach a junction that must have still been a few hundred yards away and take the left path. Another journey of what, in a dry tunnel, was about ten minutes, and he could have climbed a ladder and emerged near an old warehouse facility that was little more than a skeleton of crumbled walls and vines. That seemed so far away now.

Water rushed against and around his knees, pushing him forward. He kept one hand firmly on the wall and continued slowly and steadily onward. There were other ladders he could climb before his intended goal. He'd need to leave sooner and risk being caught.

He trudged forward, sloshing through the raging sewer river as he put as much distance between himself and the ironworks as he dared. The level had risen to just above his knees when he found a small alcove and a ladder that led to a grate.

Shane was not sure where it led. He stood beneath the grate and looked up as rainwater spattered down from a black sky. He began to climb.

The rungs of the ladder were slick with the rain and rehydrated remnants of whatever had been caked to them for years. His clothes weighed him down as he rose from the water, pulling at his legs and feet as he waited for the bulk of it to drip away and make his ascent a little easier.

Bits of filth flaked off under his hands, threatening to cost him his grip. The water roared past in a river below. Shane ignored it and climbed the last few rungs to the top of the ladder.

Water splashed into his face, a constant stream from the little rivulet in the cracked cement that led to it. It was unavoidable in the small space in which the ladder was affixed. All he could do was turn his head to breathe and spit away whatever ran down his face as he reached up blindly and pushed.

The metal held fast. He pushed harder, struggling for leverage, but nothing happened. He took another step, bending his back so his body would fit in the tighter space, and then pushed his shoulder and back up against the grate. He used the strength in his legs to push up as he straightened as much as the space would allow and tried to force the grate up. Nothing moved.

Shane pushed again, straining, and feeling the pain of the metal pushing back against his flesh. He nearly lost his footing as cakes of grime slipped off the rung under his left boot. He caught himself at the last second, holding tightly as water blasted across his face from the immovable exit.

Another curse, this one out loud, and he climbed back down. Maybe if he had the right tools and more time, he could work the grate open and get out. But he hadn't brought the pry bar with him, and the more time he wasted, the more likely he was to get caught or drown in a Vakovian sewer.

Shane dropped back into the rushing water. His knees disappeared beneath the surface. He needed a way out.

"I knew if I wanted to find a rat, I should check the sewers."

The voice barely rose above the surge of the water. Shane turned back to face the way he had come. Copland's partner, the skeletal ghost called Vox, stood in the water, barely visible in the darkness.

"Let's see if you drown like one."

CHAPTER 22

DEATH IN THE DEPTHS

Vox ran at Shane. The spirit was unfettered by the water and glided through it like it was not there. Shane braced himself as the pale ghost met him head-on and dove at him, planting a shoulder into Shane's gut.

The force of the blow along with the rush of the water was more than Shane could withstand. He fell back, reaching out for something to grab but finding nothing. Cold water washed over him, and he went under, swallowed by the deluge.

Icy hands wrapped around his throat but did not squeeze or claw. Vox was merely holding him under, his ghostly body wrapped around Shane's as he held on and tried to drown him.

Through the murk and filth, Shane caught glimpses of the ghost's face, the nightmarish visage close to his own, watching him with sadistic glee. He wanted Shane to die, and he wanted to be the one to do it. He wanted to see it happen.

Shane opened his mouth and shook his head. He ignored the taste of the water, and the rain, muck, and sewage running across his face, and clamped down on Vox's wrist. He bit as hard as he could, his teeth pushing through the papery flesh and then the bone.

Ghost flesh did not have the same resistance or texture, and bone was not as firm and real as it was in a living being. Shane chomped hard, feeling the bone compress and then splinter.

Fragments came apart in his jaws and bristled against his tongue and the roof of his mouth. The ghost bellowed in the water, the sound distorted and inhuman.

Vox pulled his arm back just as Shane rolled his body. With the surging waters pushing him along, Shane pulled away from the ghost, taking its hand with him.

For an instant, Shane was upside-down on the sewer tunnel floor, disoriented and rolling forward with the water's momentum. The ghost's hand dissolved, unable to exist apart from the whole.

Shane struggled to right himself, trying to determine which direction was up and hold still long enough to reach it. He pushed against the stony surface of the sewer tunnel with his legs and arms and rose above the waterline.

The roar of water filled his ears again and Shane spit to clear his mouth, and then gulped in a breath of air as he bobbed along with the current. There was no sign of Vox in the darkness. Shane was not sure how far downstream he had traveled or where he was.

He slowed his progress and regained his footing, a struggle that took longer than he intended. The water was midway up his thighs at that point, and the speed and force of it were much more powerful than it seemed.

Shane didn't even see the ghost come at him the second time. He was still trying to gain his footing when Vox's punch hit him in the side of the face and snapped his head left. He fell back into the stream and the ghost paced him. The handless arm hung useless at his side while his nearly lipless mouth was parted just enough to show the empty void beyond the ancient, yellowed teeth.

"I'm going to break your spine," Vox growled.

He grabbed at Shane with his one good hand but Shane batted it away and took hold of the ghost's wrist. He used it as an anchor and allowed the ghost's ability to avoid the physics of the water to brace himself.

"You seem like an angry guy," Shane sputtered, pulling himself up from the water.

Vox pulled himself free and took another swipe at Shane. Even with one hand, he knew how to fight and placed his strikes well. Someone had taught him to fight once.

Vox used his handless arm as a shield to counter blows from Shane and threw punches when and where he could. He used the blade of his hand and his elbow to strike Shane's ribs and torso as often as he aimed for his face.

Shane's body armor rendered most of the ghost's blows useless, and frustration grew on the dead man's face. He was not used to attacking a target that could counter or avoid his strikes. Most ghosts didn't have to endure the limitations of the physical world. If they wanted to kill someone, they could reach into their chest and crush their heart. Shane was not built like that. As skilled a fighter as Vox might have been, he had not had to endure an actual fight in a long time, probably the entire time he was a ghost.

For his part, Shane was hobbled by the flow of water. He could not make big moves, could not drag the ghost to the ground and fight him in close quarters with an eye to crush his skull and be done with it. Any sudden movement put him at risk of losing his footing and being swept away again.

As much as Vox was annoyed at Shane for countering his blows, it was Shane who felt pressed. He needed to keep his balance in every attack he made. It was all he could do to stay upright. An opening did not exactly give him the upper hand, and the water level was still rising.

The water was near to the top of Shane's thighs when Vox backed off the offensive. The ghost's gaze was locked on Shane and while his skeletal face betrayed little in the way of expression and what he might think, his laugh was another matter. It was a deep, clicking chuckle, slow and deliberate.

The ghost lowered his good hand to the water, letting his fingers disappear in the churning current.

"How much longer, do you think?" Vox asked.

Shane said nothing, holding his position in the tunnel. He lowered one of his hands slowly toward his pocket, not wanting a sudden movement to set the ghost off on another attack.

"Going to need you to be more specific," Shane said.

He wanted to destroy the ghost and be done with it, but the situation was quickly becoming untenable. He needed to escape the sewer, and there was no way he'd do that with Vox present. It was also unlikely he could get the edge over the ghost in the rushing water. He saw only one way out.

"How long until you can't hold that sack of meat upright anymore? How long until you become just another piece of filth washed away in this sewer? I can stay here forever," the ghost croaked.

Shane laughed and shrugged.

"What a great story that will be for you to tell. The time you got your hand bitten off, and you stood around like a bitch, waiting for sewage to win the fight for you."

Vox's eyes narrowed.

"You talk too much," he said. Shane laughed again.

"Shut me up, then."

His hand had closed around the iron knuckles in his pocket, and he slipped his fingers through the holes slowly and unnoticeably. He just needed to connect with a single punch, and the ghost could go back to Copland minus a hand. He could explain his failure while Shane found a way out.

Vox took a step forward, his good hand balled into a fist. He shifted to the left, knowing Shane was not nearly as maneuverable in the current condition.

"You can't survive this. You know that, right? Copland's going to pull your pale, bloated corpse out of this drain, and everyone's going to wonder what happened to your head. And only I am going to know," the ghost hissed.

"And you say *I* talk too much," Shane said.

Vox growled and took a step forward. Shane pulled the iron knuckles from his pocket.

"You're not falling for that, are you Vox?"

A second ghost joined them, coming up behind the pale-skinned one in the dark. Vox turned to face the spirit that Shane recognized from back in Nashua. The burned ghost at the diner with Blakely. The burned ghost who had murdered him.

"I don't need help," Vox said, ignoring the other spirit. The burned one grinned and looked at Shane, his eyes dropping to the iron knuckles.

"No? Looks like you're about to get dropped like a bad habit. Can't stop showboating long enough to get a job done, huh?"

"No one asked you, Dell," Vox raged, turning on the newcomer and pushing him against the sewer wall with his good hand. "What are you even doing here?"

"Looking for you," Dell replied. "Been gone so long, Copland wanted me to make sure you didn't get popped like a balloon down here."

"He's not going to kill me," Vox said, glaring at Shane.

"No, I'm just pulling pieces off him. Figure if I hollow him out, I can use him as a boat," Shane added.

Dell laughed and Vox growled, pushing the new ghost back down the tunnel away from him.

"He's mine."

"Then stop wasting time. Copland's getting antsy."

"Copland can wait," Vox said.

The water had risen above Shane's thighs and would reach his waist soon enough. He backed away slowly, watching the ghosts and keeping the iron knuckles at the ready. The distance between himself and wherever their haunted items were had to be significant by now. They would not find him again if they lost him, and they knew it.

"Where the hell are you going?" the skeletal ghost asked, noticing that Shane was putting distance between them.

"Trying to leave, honestly."

He could hear something in the distance now, a different tone to the water somewhere in the tunnel ahead. The noise ahead was deeper, louder, and faster. He knew what it meant if he could reach it. It was going to be a furious rush, two tunnels merging as one and dumping twice the water with twice the force. He could lose the ghosts there or die. There weren't a lot of other options.

"Just kill him already," Dell said. "Or let me do it."

"No!" Vox shouted, pushing the other ghost away. "He's mine."

Shane turned from the two spirits and dove. The current swept him up quickly, and he rode it forward, arm over arm, swimming with it wherever it took him.

Vox screamed behind him, a bellow of frustrated rage followed by the laughter of the other ghost. Shane did not look back, not that he could have even if he wanted to. The current was impossible to fight.

Instead of trying to work against the water, Shane worked with it. He kept his head above water when he could, coasting along as the roar of the joining tunnel grew louder. It felt like he was rushing headlong into a lion's mouth, but the alternative was just as bad. He could not fight two ghosts in the flooded sewer, and he would have died if he'd stayed.

He heard Vox howling as the ghost tried to keep pace with him. The current was swift, and even a ghost could not hope to keep up. Soon, the ghost's frustrated cries were overwhelmed by the rush of water from the new tunnel.

Shane prepared himself as best as he could, but the darkness of the sewer made it feel like he was being swallowed by a void. There was nothing to see; he could only feel the rumble grow more powerful, filling his head with the sound of ceaseless power.

After a moment, he was tossed end over end as if he'd been hit by a truck. His arms and legs scraped against the sewer walls and floor and any sense of up or down was lost.

He struggled to right himself, to find a smooth way to move with the current, but it was nearly impossible. The water churned and battered and pushed him about. At some point, he found himself on the surface again, gasping for breaths that still came with mouthfuls of water until he retched.

He was nearly at the tunnel's ceiling now, and he could find no footing. He had no idea whether the ladder he intended to use as an escape had come and gone. He was moving at a furious pace with no sense of direction.

There was nothing he could do to save himself any longer. Nothing to hold on to or slow his progress. He did not know where the tunnel headed, where or how it ended.

The water level rose until there were moments when a surge or push would raise Shane to the ceiling and scrape his flesh against the stone. He kept his hands up, to brace himself and prevent his face from being scraped from his skull. The tradeoff was that he had to push beneath the water to do so.

Something in the sound of the water's roar was changing again. He could not put his finger on what it was this time: Struggling to simply stay above the water and stay alive was all he could do. But something was coming. He could feel it.

If the tunnels merged again, if another was going to add its flow to the one in which he was already trapped, it would be all over. There was no more room. There would be no chance of survival.

The pitch rose and Shane gritted his teeth, waiting for the water to push to the roof of the tunnel. The speed seemed to increase, and now, it felt as much like he was being pulled as pushed. The water level decreased, and he realized it was harder to touch the ceiling.

But if the water was draining, that meant it was going somewhere.

CHAPTER 23
REBORN

The sense that the bottom of the world had fallen out suddenly gripped Shane. No longer was he being pushed forward; he was being pulled down. The tunnel had ended. Water gushed like a geyser, and Shane was vomited from the sewer out into the open.

He saw distant lights for a moment, and a flash of lightning in the sky that turned the world blue-white. There was only a moment to register the choppy surface of a massive pool coming toward him before he splashed into it, plunging headfirst under the surface.

The water was warmer than what he'd just come from. He floated weightlessly for a moment, feeling the churning of the pipe spilling onto his back even several feet below the surface, before he kicked and pumped his arms, struggling up toward the air.

The sound of water splashing was still loud but nowhere near as all-consuming as the roar in the tunnel. Shane turned in place, treading water, and looked back. The sewer tunnel jutted out of the side of a hill and was spilling into a pond.

The sky above was still stormy, but not as powerful as before. Rain fell gently, and when the lightning flashed, he could see the shoreline nearby. Dirt and trees and shrubs. From his vantage point, he could see no sign of the city.

He swam to shore, pulling himself out of the water and feeling a hundred pounds heavier. With a grunt, he slumped to the dirt and lay there, letting the water drain away as he stared up at the black sky.

He must have traveled right to the edge of the city, to a storm runoff site meant to handle flooding. He was well past his intended goal. That was fine, though. It meant he would probably be well past where police might look for him. And well beyond the reach of Vox and Dell, at least for a time.

Shane stayed on the shore with rain pelting his face for a long while. Too long, he realized. Despite everything, he thought he could have fallen asleep there. His body had been put through the wringer, and he felt it fighting against him, wanting to rest and relax. But it was not an option.

He forced himself to sit up and then cautiously got to his feet, trying to get the lay of the land. The pond was in a depression, and the land around it rose into a small hill on all sides. He climbed, sticking to shrubs and trees for cover until he crested the rise.

The city of Ravjek was still close—he could see the buildings and lights—but he was a good distance from it. When the lightning flashed, he could see the smoke billowing from the ironworks well over a mile away.

Directly ahead at the end of a road sat what looked like a small warehouse with a handful of cars in a parking lot. It was perhaps a hundred yards away and lit by a single light above a door.

Shane crept down the hill and made his way toward the warehouse. No one was around that he could see. He stayed out of sight of any potential cameras or security guards that might have been patrolling the area, crouching at the edge of the rusty fence that surrounded the lot.

Nothing moved for a long time, just the now-far-less-intense rain. Shane quickly climbed the fence and dropped into the lot, dashing to the nearest of the cars. It was an ugly silver two-door with mismatched doors. He tried the handle, found it locked, and gave the driver's-side window a quick punch with the iron knuckles. Glass shattered, raining shards into the car.

He unlocked the door and wiped off the seat, then pried open the steering column to access the wires inside. The car was from the mid-eighties from the look of it. It had been some time since Shane had hotwired a car, but it wasn't hard to remember which wire went where.

The engine rumbled to life and Shane pulled the door shut, quickly putting the car into gear. He was not sure where he was or where he was going, but he could work that out on the road. He pulled out of the lot with the car's lights off and drove several blocks before turning them on.

Vox and Dell would have already reported back to Copland. He would know Shane was still alive. If Shane were in Copland's shoes, he would change his mission to accommodate for that information and up the timetable for their assassination of Zemba.

In talking with Vanko, Shane had learned that Zemba was far from a mysterious figure that was hard to reach. He was President Janosik's only opposition and a well-known public figure, but he avoided Ravjek because of the attempts made on his life. His closest ally fell out of a window the day he arrived in Ravjek the year prior, and no one doubted who was behind it.

Janosik had likely called on the Reapers to take out Zemba to at least have the air of legitimacy. If it looked like someone else had killed him, then Janosik had plausible deniability. Even if everyone knew he was behind it, no one would be able to prove it.

Shane didn't need to find Copland, he needed to find Zemba. Copland would come for a kill. He'd be prepared to take out not just Zemba but whatever security he had with him, which had to be significant. That's where Copland would be next. Vox and Dell would be there, too. He could get all three in one place at the same time if he was smart about it. But it was not something he could manage on his own.

Shane drove into the city. He didn't want to risk being caught again, but he had no choice, and one last play to make. A pit stop was all he needed.

He returned to Vanko's bar and parked in the back where he had taken the car from Vanko's cousin earlier. It was late, and the bar was closed, but a light came on when Shane knocked on the back door. He waited five minutes before the barrel of a gun came through a small hole at chest level.

"Is very late for visitors," Vanko said.

"I missed you; what can I say?" Shane replied. There was a pause and then laughter from inside as the gun was pulled away.

"American! I thought you'd be dead by now," Vanko said, opening the door. "You look like hell."

"Do I?" Shane asked. He'd caught a quick glimpse in the rearview mirror on the drive over. Scrapes from the sewer wall across his face were shallow but wide, like brush burn, and made it look like he'd sanded off part of his face.

"You're sopping wet. Did you swim here?" the Russian asked when Shane stepped inside.

"Part of the way, yes," Shane said.

Vanko had a cigar lit and was wearing a robe. He turned on a light and was about to offer Shane a seat then thought better of it.

"What do you need?"

"Just information," Shane said. "Where can I find Peter Zemba?"

Vanko raised his eyebrows and grunted around his cigar.

"Zemba now? Are you planning a countercoup?"

"Trying to save his life," Shane replied. "Silvershore consultants are working for Janosik to assassinate Zemba and keep his hands clean. They're going to make their move on Zemba soon. If not tonight, then tomorrow. I need to get there first."

"This is culmination of your vengeance plot in Vakovia?" Vanko asked, chewing on the cigar.

"It's what got two of my friends killed. I'd like to stop Copland before he gets everything he wants."

The Russian stopped his chewing and stared at Shane in silence.

"What?" Shane asked, feeling the tension from the other man.

"Copland?" Vanko asked. "Lt. Colonel Joseph Copland?"

He enunciated the words very carefully, and Shane nodded.

"He has run Silvershore since he killed Blakely. He's gunning for Zemba."

Vanko took the cigar from his mouth, holding it between two fingers as he pointed at Shane.

"You never say Copland before. You never say his name!"

"You know him?"

Vanko growled and mashed his cigar into an ashtray.

"I know Lt. Colonel Joseph Copland, yes. My brother knew him. My cousin, Dmitri, knew him. They are dead now. Strike in Azerbaijan fifteen years ago. Ordered by Copland based on wrong intelligence. Wrong intelligence!"

He got to his feet, and for a moment, it seemed like he was going to punch Shane. Instead, he turned away and put his fist through a wall, the drywall crumbling around his wrist as he pulled it back out again, blood on his knuckles.

"He has been here in Vakovia? For how long?"

"As long as Silvershore has been here, I think."

"I will kill him myself. I know the office, American. Come with me; we will tear it down around his ears and stomp his skull into the ruins."

Shane had not seen Vanko so animated before. If he had not been so enraged, it might have been funny.

"We can't," Shane said.

"Why?" the Russian slapped the desk. "I am owed vengeance, too. My family is owed!"

"I already destroyed the office. Blew it up."

Vanko stared blankly at him.

"You blew it up?"

"The RPG you sold me."

The Russian's face split open in a grin as he began to laugh.

"You blew it up!"

He slapped the desk again, less angry this time and more caught up in the mirth of his enemy's loss.

"Vanko, I need to know where to find Zemba. That's the only place we'll find Copland now. If Zemba dies, Silvershore's contract in Vakovia will be closed, and he'll move on. Or start hunting me. Or both. I have a small window here."

The Russian let his laughter continue for a while longer as he nodded and took a deep breath.

"Okay, American. Okay. I want this Copland, but if he is looking for Zemba... I cannot go on such short notice. Zemba is not in Ravjek. He works out of Seeburg, in the south. It is where Janosik has the least influence and support. It is not short trip."

"How far?" Shane asked.

"By car? Roads are unpredictable, many closures and detours from damage never repaired. I have not made the trip in years. Could take four hours. Could take eight."

"No idea on the best route?"

"Best route ten years ago? Today? Only a guess."

He began rifling through drawers in cabinets, pulling out books and papers until he came across a pocket-sized book of maps. He opened it and flipped through the pages until he found what he was looking for.

"Here," Vanko said. "Book was published in... eh, nineteen ninety-five. Is good enough."

He used a pen from the desk and traced a track from one point to another then handed it to Shane. The map was small, but the roads were at least labeled.

"You need gun? Another RPG?" Vanko asked. Shane shook his head. He had no time to wait for supplies, and a gun would do nothing in a fight against Vox and Dell.

"No. Thank you for this, Vanko. I have to go," he said.

"Take gas cans in parking lot," the Russian said. "Enough to reach

Seeburg, I'm sure. Gas stations on road are unreliable."

Shane nodded and headed back out the door into the night. Vanko watched him as he loaded two gas cans from next to the fence into the trunk of his stolen car.

"You kill Copland, and we're even for gas and map," the Russian said. Shane laughed and got into the car.

"You have a deal." Shane twisted the wires to start the engine again. He pulled out of the lot and returned to the road heading south.

Ravjek was in his rearview mirror within minutes.

CHAPTER 24

THE LONG ROAD AHEAD

The southern road was nearly identical to the road that had led Shane to Kogar. The sheer number of dead was unreasonable, but after what he'd seen, not unexpected. So many of the dead in Vakovia had returned. He wondered what triggered it. The only thing that made sense was the scale of it. The slaughter en masse.

War had visited this part of the world for generations. Before it was called Vakovia, before there was democracy or anything pretending to be it, this was a land of turmoil dating back centuries. Shane was not sure when the land had last known peace.

As much as Shane knew about the dead, he knew it almost all on an individual level. He knew ghosts like Carl and Herbert and Eloise. He knew the fundamentals of how they worked, of a haunted item binding a soul, of salt keeping it hidden, or iron forcing it away. But the in-depth stuff, or the reasons behind it, were mysteries.

Was there science to life after death? A recipe for how to make a ghost? Vakovia seemed to have locked it down, but the cost might have been dire. Maybe it was generation after generation of trauma and suffering. Maybe death had seeped into the land like water into sand and was just a part of it now. Maybe coming back in Vakovia was all but unavoidable.

Shane drove down a once-paved road that had long ago fallen into disrepair and was now like an extremely uneven dirt road. An SUV or truck would have handled it far better than his stolen two-door, but he would make do.

He passed some abandoned structures, but there was more life here as well. He passed small hamlets and villages, mostly asleep and silent, with a few lights and the odd living face that saw him pass alongside the spirits.

He reached his first roadblock after an hour of driving, when the road was meant to continue over a bridge that no longer existed. The river, fat with rainwater, raged along flooded shores. The ends of the bridge were still visible on either side of the water, but the rust and age made it look like the structure had collapsed years ago.

Shane returned to the small book of maps Vanko had provided and looked for the closest alternative route. He would need to drive west a distance, but there was always a chance he'd find a road that the map hadn't included and get back on track sooner.

The new route took Shane off paved roads and down dirt tracks with weeds growing in the center. He rumbled along the uneven ground and watched as ghosts on the roadside stared at him as he passed. Some waved in greeting, others scowled, and many more remained blank-faced and disinterested.

Miles had passed under the wheels of his stolen car when he came upon another village. This one bore signs of life as a few lights burned in windows and a man sat in a chair on his porch drinking from a mug as Shane drove by. A ghost stood mere feet away from him, and Shane was not sure the man knew it was there.

He saw curtains sway in a window as he drove past a large farmhouse and wondered if Copland might have left men out in the country to watch for Shane. Zemba could also have had his forces scattered across the countryside. If people were trying to kill him, it would be good to have an early warning of someone approaching.

Shane hoped he hadn't triggered any countermeasures by driving straight to his destination. If anything, he should have made them curious about who he was and what he was doing. His car was the sort of vehicle a potential assassin would have chosen to navigate the rough countryside.

The rain had stopped part of the way through the journey, and the clouds had passed, revealing a blanket of stars. Away from Ravjek and all signs of humanity, far from any lights, the Vakovian countryside was almost like another world.

Shane remembered one such night when he was still in the Marines. Under a clear sky, far from the city, and trying to make it through the night without being shot by someone he couldn't see.

"We could die out here, and no one would ever know what happened," Blakely had said at the time. They were in the desert, monitoring the movements of insurgents, and the sky was so clear that it revealed the faint wash of the Milky Way.

"They'd know. Someone would file a report," Shane told him.

"No, man! I mean it. If we never reported in, if the whole unit gets taken out, how would anyone know? They'd look for us, find bodies, and maybe put puzzle pieces together, but that's not what I mean. No one knows the true story of the dead, Ryan. No one but them."

It had meant little to Shane at the time. Marines sometimes talked some crazy talk in the middle of the night. Looking back, maybe it was a little more. If Blakely could see the dead back then, and talk to them, maybe he already had the wheels turning for his Silvershore endeavor.

Shane had never seen a spirit around his friend, but some were always nearby, even out in the desert. Wanderers, lost souls, and random spirits that never seemed to have a place were always around in war.

His thoughts were interrupted upon seeing the road ahead of him was too badly damaged to continue down. He was forced to make another detour then, and then another, when the road just stopped. Shane had to get out of his car to check, but the path simply vanished after hitting a crossroads when the map said it should have continued. It must have taken years of disuse or some intentional effort to remove the road, but it was gone.

Shane decided to just keep driving in the general direction to Seeburg.

After half an hour, he found a road that wasn't on the map. It was barely a single lane of unpaved dirt that cut through the countryside, but it showed signs of use. He drove as quickly as he dared along the meandering path that circled trees and led through an unusually hilly patch of countryside that blocked much of what lay ahead from view.

When he found himself around the trees, Shane was greeted by the sight of distant lights. A town waited for him, what he hoped was Seeburg, despite there being no signs.

His trip had taken six hours. The town of Seeburg was not nearly as large as Ravjek from what Shane could see, but it was not a tiny village of a handful of houses, either. If anything, the closer he got, the more it looked like a gated community from the suburbs. Or a prison.

Shane stopped a suitable distance from the border of where he was headed. He no longer had binoculars or any supplies besides what was on him, but he could see a guard fence and light towers from a distance.

Men stood on tall, wooden towers at either corner of a gate to enter the town. It was not a sealed gate that barred entry, just a monitored one. Shane wondered if the town had just taken Zemba in. Perhaps it was his home originally, and they had adapted to extra security to ensure the man's safety.

From end to end, the fence was not any great distance, maybe enough to cover several normal city blocks. There was no way to see how deep the town extended beyond that, but Shane couldn't imagine Seeburg was home to more than a few hundred homes.

The fence and towers did not look old, nor did they look entirely professional. The towers were constructed from wood but had the look of something done by people used to raising barns. Efficient and well made, but also homemade. This was a small group of people trying to protect themselves.

It was too far to make out clear details, but Shane assumed the men were armed. There was likely some kind of an alert system as well to send word if people like Copland were coming. None of it would matter when he came, though. Vox and Dell and the other ghosts would kill any guards, silence the alarms, and destroy whatever got in their way.

Vox could go in alone and kill Zemba if they knew where he was, but Shane did not think that was the plan. Copland might kill some lower-level security that way, but Zemba himself? Copland would want to be there, if not to pull the trigger, then at least to watch. He hadn't needed to be present for Blakely's death, but he was. He enjoyed death. The relative stillness of the town meant Shane had arrived first.

He drove the car off the road and into the nearby shrubs, leaving it covered and obscured from view. There had to be better roads to Seeburg than the one he took, but if anyone followed his tracks or was looking from town, he wanted to at least make it hard to discern he was there.

Shane needed to find Zemba and warn him, but realistically, no one was going to let him into that town. An American, a retired Marine, coming in at dawn in a bulletproof vest? He looked like he was what he was warning against.

For Zemba to have bothered to put up a fence and guard towers meant his security had been a longstanding issue, and everything Shane had heard supported that. Janosik wanted the man dead, and there must have been several prior attempts on his life. If Shane could even survive long enough to reach the gate, they'd never let him speak to Zemba in person. At least not before it was too late.

Raiding a fortified town had not been Shane's plan, but his hands were tied. He stayed off the road and crept along through the countryside, using the trees for cover as he scouted the town and looked for the best opening.

A hundred yards from where he'd left the car, he found a large tree and paused there to get his bearings, straining to see the fence and where guards had set up positions. The townspeople had cut down even the shrubs around the town and there was no cover closer than where Shane was.

"*Ideš sa vplížiť?*"

Shane looked up at the source of the voice. The ghost of a child sat on a branch of the tree. The boy was dressed in dirty clothes, peppered with holes and tears, and the skin on his face was covered in small sores.

"Sorry, my Slovak's a little rusty," Shane said. The boy jumped down next to him.

"You sneak in?" he asked in English.

"Ideally," Shane said, not paying the boy that much attention, his eyes still locked on the fence. "You know a way?"

"I know all the ways. Are you here to kill Mr. Zemba?"

Now Shane looked at the ghost. The boy's eyes had narrowed, and the cool air radiated off him.

"The opposite. I'm trying to stop someone from killing him with ghosts. Problem is they'll never believe me, so I need to sneak in and get to him before the ghosts get here."

"That is problem," the boy agreed. "You can go there."

He pointed at the fence, at nowhere in particular, and Shane shook his head, squinting to see anything that was different.

"Where?"

"Yellow building. No window. You see?" the ghost said. Shane could see a faded yellow structure near the fence line. The fence was exposed, with no cover anywhere leading to that point.

"Zemba is staying there?" he asked incredulously.

"No, but you follow the path going to yellow building to get inside."

"There's no cover," Shane told the ghost. The boy didn't have to worry about cover; no one could see him. Maybe he was too young to understand.

"Ground is cover. Look," the boy explained, pointing, and waving his one finger from side to side. "Look at... swoop?"

Shane tried to track what the boy was saying. The lighting was poor, but he saw a clear shadow in the center of the ground, untouched by the fence lights, leading up to the yellow structure.

"A depression," Shane said, though "swoop" seemed reasonable enough. There was a low point in the ground, almost like a gully, that dipped below where the light touched. He would have to crawl, but it extended right to the fence.

"Thanks," Shane said to the ghost. The boy smiled and was already up in the tree again.

"If you kill Mr. Zemba, I kill you," the ghost replied. "He is nice man."

Shane grunted and headed toward the gully, staying low to the ground.

Fair enough, he thought.

CHAPTER 25

DEATH AND THE REAPERS

The gully must have once been a stream or at least a drainage ditch. Shane army-crawled through the shadow-shrouded ravine, out of sight from both sides to anyone not standing directly over him, and made his way to the fence's edge.

As expected, the fence was simple and hastily erected. It was just a regular chain link, the kind people in the suburbs would use to keep their dogs in the yard. Shane popped the simple metal brackets that held the links to the nearest post until he could pull it up enough to slip under and into the town.

The chain rattled softly, but he moved quickly. He could see no one nearby, and he hoped no one heard as he crawled into the shadows of the windowless, yellow building.

The sun would be up soon. Shane crept to the front of the building and looked out at the street. There were nondescript houses in both directions. Cars were parked on the streets. The buildings were designed in much the same manner, with high-peaked roofs, red shingles, and muted siding in white or yellow or gray. A few were pink.

The streets were made of well-maintained cobblestone. There were a few scattered trees along the sidewalks, but little green otherwise. It looked like a regular town where regular people lived.

The ghosts of Seeburg were fewer in number than their counterparts in the country, or at least they were staying out of sight. Shane saw a lone ghost walking the sidewalk with his head down. His clothes made him look like he'd stepped out of World War II.

Zemba had to be in a fortified area. Whatever building had the most security would likely be his. Even though Seeburg was a small town, it wasn't so small that he could run from house to house to track the man down in a matter of minutes.

Shane moved from the yellow building to the next, staying in the shadows and moving swiftly. The sky was lightening, and the first signs of life were appearing. A car drove down the street, and a man on a bicycle passed closely enough that if he'd turned and looked, he would have had to have seen Shane.

This is not a good idea, Shane thought, taking a deep breath. He stripped off his vest and tossed it between the yellow house and its neighbor, then used the inside of his shirt to clean his face of any mud.

A black T-shirt and black pants did not look too suspicious, or he hoped they didn't. He left the cover of the shadows and walked casually to the sidewalk and then started on his way down the street.

The sun rose and more people left their homes. Men, women, and children went about their day, some driving and others walking. Children headed toward a large schoolhouse not far from where Shane had entered the town. Others chatted with friends on their lawns while most vehicles headed in the same direction, toward the center of town.

Shane followed the flow of traffic. He kept his pace casual and only a few people bothered to give him a second glance. His clothing was not a perfect match for anyone in town, but enough others wore simple T-shirts or dark pants that he was not an eyesore.

By the time he reached what qualified as Seeburg's downtown, the sun was up, the sky was clear, and the town was awake. Like Ravjek, there was an outdoor market, though this one was considerably smaller. The smells of fresh-baked bread and spices filled the air, and a crowd of people shopped and talked and ate all around him.

Beyond the market, a series of old military Jeeps were parked outside a large, white building that could have been an apartment or an office. A much smaller crowd was gathered outside, with men and women crowded around a trio of men on the building's steps.

Shane took an apple from a basket on a table and handed the vendor an American twenty-dollar bill. He walked toward the Jeeps and the small crowd, eating the apple while trying to hear over the din of the market behind him.

A woman was speaking Hungarian, and another was talking over her in Polish. One of the three men in the center, a man about Shane's age wearing a light sweater and brown pants, was trying to appease them both, smiling and using his hands to signal for them to calm down. He had the mannerisms of a politician.

Shane joined the crowd, eating his apple and listening in. He was catching up mid-conversation, but it seemed like the women were arguing over supplies that were needed, bulk items not found in the market.

"I am doing my best," the man in the center replied in Polish. "The trucks will no longer come to Seeburg, but I have been talking to officials in Romania."

"It's not fair, Peter," the Hungarian woman said. "It is not your burden."

"And it is not yours, Ilona," the man replied.

Shane chewed his apple. If this was Peter Zemba, it was almost frightening how easy it was for Shane to reach him. Security was present outside, but inside, anybody could approach him. Copland would have him dead before the man had his morning coffee.

"Peter Zemba?" Shane asked as the man finished with the two women. It looked like he had been on his way to the white building but stopped momentarily to address the women's concerns.

The two men with Zemba tensed, their eyes locked on Shane. They were armed, and the nearest of them had his hands on the weapon holstered in his jacket.

"Yes. And you are not Polish, are you?" the man replied in Polish, eyeing Shane. Zemba had curly brown hair and a series of scars up one side of his face that looked several years old, pale and glossy against the rest of his ruddier flesh. He was not a physically imposing man, and perhaps his only noteworthy feature was his green eyes which were clear and bright and didn't waver when they caught someone's gaze.

"No," Shane admitted, speaking Polish as well.

"American?" Zemba guessed. Shane nodded and finished his apple.

"I am."

"How did he get here?" the man on Zemba's right asked the man on his left in Russian.

"Under the fence," Shane replied in the same language.

The men pulled their guns now, and Shane raised his hands, holding up his apple core.

"If I was here to cause trouble, I wouldn't have brought fruit," he explained.

"You have a knife," one man said, nodding to Shane's belt.

"So do fishermen. I need to talk to you, Mr. Zemba," Shane said, returning to Polish. "Someone is coming to kill you."

"On your knees," one of Zemba's bodyguards said, approaching Shane and pressing the barrel of his gun to Shane's temple.

"Gregor, enough," Zemba said, waving his man off before Shane had a chance to move. Zemba looked Shane up and down while Gregor took Shane's Kabar and patted him down, finding the iron knuckles as well.

"What is your name?" Zemba asked.

"Shane Ryan," he answered. "There's a man named Joseph Copland who runs a group called Silvershore. President Janosik hired them to kill you and your men. His original plan was to do it when you get to Ravjek, but I think he's coming here today."

Zemba blinked, pursed his lips, and nodded.

"Well. Isn't that something," he said with a chuckle. "And why would he change his plan and kill me today?"

"I tried to blow him up last night and failed. He's really pissed off."

Zemba laughed loudly.

"I see. I have heard of this Copland, you know. And I know Silvershore well. Their leader was killed not so long ago."

"Davis Blakely. Murdered in Kogar, where he thought he was meeting you."

Zemba's smile was gone now.

"I never met this man," he said seriously. Shane nodded.

"Copland set it up. Murdered him and told the others it was your doing. Made international news."

"And gives sympathy to Janosik," Zemba said.

"Politics is your business, but Blakely was a friend of mine. Copland killed him to take control and to get paid. I missed my chance last night, but I don't plan to let him succeed today. And he will succeed if you're not ready."

"Mr. Ryan, give me some credit. I have survived this long and—"

The sound of a gunshot cut Zemba off before he could finish his sentence. Blood sprayed across the man's surprised face. Screams erupted in the market as one of the two bodyguards fell, a hole in his chest.

Someone in the building behind them shouted and windows broke. Shane pushed Zemba to the ground and scrambled behind one of the Jeeps with him as more shots rang out.

The market erupted into a frenzy of people running for their lives. Gunfire echoed off the buildings, now being returned from Zemba's side. He had security on the roof and in the windows of the building, taking shots at whoever was firing in their direction. Shane looked out from behind one of the Jeep tires and waited for another shot, tracing it back with his eyes to the roof of a building to the left of the market.

"Rooftop. Yellow building with the white trim, west of the market by the bread vendor," Shane said to Gregor, who was huddled with him and Zemba. The man stared at Shane for a moment before relaying the information over a radio.

"Your timing is impeccable, Mr. Ryan," Zemba said, cleaning the blood from his face with the sleeve of his sweater.

"We need to get you someplace out of sight," Shane told him. "The shooters aren't what you need to worry about."

"What does that mean?" Zemba asked.

"Highly skilled assassins that will get past your security if they haven't already."

An explosion drowned out the end of what Shane was saying. Debris rained down on them as one of the Jeeps was torn apart in a burst of fire and metal.

Shane pulled on Zemba, dragging him up the stairs to the entrance of the building moments before the Jeep behind which they'd been hiding exploded as well. Copland had taken a page from Shane's book and was firing RPGs.

Metal and stone rained down as fire licked at their heels. The force of the blast knocked both men forward, and Shane felt small pieces of shrapnel sear into his back.

Security inside the building was returning fire from the door and encouraging Zemba to get to them. One man opened fire, spraying the market and anything beyond with bullets while another crawled to Shane and Zemba.

"Head out the back," Shane said, gripping Zemba's arm as he crawled away.

"What?"

"This building will not save you. Head out the rear and run. You need to get at least a mile away."

"I need—"

"At least a mile or you are a dead man," Shane said with as much gravity as he could muster. Zemba stared at Shane, his eyes boring into Shane's, and he nodded.

"One mile," he mumbled.

"As fast as you can."

Zemba scrambled into the building and his security slammed heavy doors shut behind him. Gunfire from the building kept Copland's forces pinned down, but the return fire had killed a dozen civilians or more, plus several of Zemba's security forces.

The rooftop shooter had not fired a round in some time. Zemba's forces might have stopped him, but there were at least two more still firing. He needed to find an opening and move when he could.

"Looks like the sewer rat got away."

Shane looked up as Vox approached him.

"Wondered when you were going to show up," Shane said. The ghost's leathery flesh split in a macabre smile.

"I'm going to enjoy watching you bleed."

CHAPTER 26
WARLORD

Shane's foot connected with the ghost's knee before he had a chance to say or do anything else. Vox's leg bent backward, and the ghost howled as Shane lunged at him. His leg was broken but Shane needed the ghost gone entirely. He'd had his fill of him in the sewer.

The ghost collapsed onto the steps, and Shane was on him in seconds. He took the dead man's ankle in hand and rolled his body in a swift, smooth motion, breaking the appendage free from Vox's body.

Vox roared rage and frustration, and Shane drove an elbow into his face, shattering the teeth in his lipless mouth. The ghost pushed him off and stood, scrambling on his half-leg and falling forward as gunshots rang out around them.

"No!" the ghost shouted, using his one good hand to prop himself up on his one good knee. His eyes were fixed on Shane with a glare of hatred, and though it felt petty on some level, Shane was immensely satisfied.

"You're shorter than I remember," Shane said, staying low to avoid the Reapers' gunfire.

Vox came for him again, scrambling like a beast now. Shane repositioned, moving up several steps, and kicked out. His boot took Vox in the face with enough force to offset the ghost's jaw.

A bullet hit the steps next to Shane's hand, and he was forced to descend again, attacking the ghost directly once more by tackling him. He reached a hand into the ghost's mouth, grasping the now-broken jaw and pulling it away from his skull. It released with a popping sound and dissolved in his hand.

Vox gurgled and wailed but could no longer speak. He reached for Shane's throat with his good hand and squeezed, the icy fingers digging into the flesh with a biting cold.

Shane held the ghost's wrist with one hand and with his free arm thrust upward, snapping Vox's elbow. Bestial howls came from his jawless mouth, and Shane ripped his forearm free from the broken joint.

The ghost fell over and then propped himself up on the stump where he'd lost his other hand. Shane had reduced him to almost nothing. He could barely move, could not take hold of anything, and could not even speak. Only his eyes could show the rage seething within him.

Another explosion rocked the market, and one of the Reapers ran from his position, his body engulfed in flames. More of Zemba's security had arrived from the rear and Copland's forces were now flanked and pinned down.

"Best of luck," Shane said to Vox, leaving him struggling where he was. He could have finished him off—maybe even should have—but Shane wanted Copland before he got to Zemba, and wasting time with Vox would not accomplish that.

He ducked around the building while the remaining Reapers stayed out of sight. By Shane's estimation, there were only two left, including Copland, but he didn't know where.

Shane ran along the side of the building toward where he'd told Zemba to go. He reached the rear and found two dead guards on the ground, and across the next cobblestone street, a single figure running toward the buildings there.

"Dell," Shane shouted. The ghost stopped and looked back at him, the burned face curving into a smile.

"Vox didn't get you yet?" the ghost shouted across the road. They walked slowly toward one another. No one was on the street, and the town of Seeburg had gone into hiding to wait out the chaos.

"He tried. Give him an hour, and he might be able to crawl to this side of the building," Shane replied.

"Cold," Dell said with some appreciation. "I'm surprised Blakely was your friend."

"Yeah?" Shane asked. The ghost shrugged.

"You've got that killer instinct. He didn't."

"Why'd you kill him?" Shane asked.

Dell grinned widely and the black, cracked flesh of his burns split open, showing glistening, red meat within.

"Who says I killed him?"

"The ghosts of Kogar."

"God," Dell said, shaking his head. "You talked to them too, huh? You're a busy little beaver. Listen, whatever, who cares? I killed him. I ripped a hole right through his chest. He was giving up. He lost the thrill, you know?"

"No," Shane said. They were face to face on the street now.

"I signed up for this to kill," Dell growled. "These burns? Goddamn white phosphorus. War crime stuff. I came back to get my shot. To have my chance to show them what it feels like to stare down death and have no escape, and I was not going to let Blakely bitch out on me."

Shane's fist landed with a thump. Dell stumbled, stunned by the unexpected attack, and the second punch knocked him over.

"You guys always have the worst stories," Shane said, dropping a knee to the ghost's gut. He punched him again and again, slamming his head into the cobblestones. "I'd kick my own ass before I stand here and listen to whatever sob story you're trying to tell me."

There would be no great lesson learned about Blakely's death. It was not profound or significant. The ghost had killed him for the same selfish, myopic reasons a hundred other murders were committed each day. It was pointless, but at least Shane could get some closure on it.

Dell's head squished against the stone as Shane pressed his weight on it. He squeezed and pushed as the ghost struggled.

"Wait! Wait, I can help you! I can tell you about Copland," Dell begged.

"I'll figure it out on my own," Shane replied. He lurched forward with his entire weight. The ghost's skull buckled and then popped open.

The blast rolled over Shane like another RPG going off. He was tossed back and rolled uncomfortably to his side, coughing, and feeling the wave of pain cross over every inch of him like he'd received a full-body kick.

In the buildings beyond him, a pained yell was cut off abruptly like someone clamped their mouth shut to muffle it. Shane scanned the area as he sat up, his eyes falling on the narrow passage between two houses in which something moved among the shadows.

Shane was back on his feet as quickly as he could manage. He loped across the remainder of the street and ducked into the narrow alley, approaching the figure that lay there in the darkness. Not a ghost this time, but a man dressed in black.

"Copland," Shane yelled, approaching the older man. He was on his back, staring up at the patch of sky visible between the buildings above them and struggling to breathe.

The left side of his torso was exposed, and the armor he wore was open. and his gut was bleeding, as was a portion of his thigh. His pants had been torn away down to the knee.

"God, I hate you," the colonel muttered.

"You had it in your pocket," Shane said, looking at the man's torn pants. He'd been carrying Dell's haunted item and watching from the shadows to see if the ghost would kill Shane. Just like he'd watched him kill Blakely.

"I should have killed you in my office. I should have killed you day one," Copland said, his voice strained and breathy.

The wound in his side was deep. Shane could see something embedded in it, a piece of metal that was twisted and dark.

"Combat knife?" Shane asked. Dell's haunted item had been the knife he'd used when he was alive. Might have been the last thing he held before the phosphorus did him in.

"Should have gutted you on the damn floor," the other man continued.

"Zemba's alive," Shane pointed out. "So Janosik won't get what he wants, either. Looks like Silvershore's a failure across the board, Copland. You can go down in history as a mercenary and a killer, just like the rest of Reaper Company."

Copland wheezed and looked at Shane. He smiled, blood between his teeth, and laughed.

"Janosik? You're a simple one, aren't you Ryan? You and Blakely both."

He laughed again and wheezed more as the movement caused excess blood to flow from his wound. Shane leaned forward, looking down at him.

"You're not working for Janosik?"

"You think the President of Vakovia can afford Reapers? This country is a dump, Ryan. Poor and pathetic."

"Then who? Why?"

"It was never about Vakovia. And I'll tell you something else, Ryan. You hear that?"

He lifted a hand unsteadily, pointing to the sky. Shane tilted his head and, distant but growing closer, the sound of helicopter blades filled the air.

"Extraction team?" Shane asked.

"Reaper Company isn't one squad," Copland hissed. "It's Reaper *Company*, Ryan. A whole damn company. They're coming. Not for Zemba this time. They're coming for you."

Shane stood up as the helicopter grew louder. Copland continued to laugh.

"They have your face. They have your name. You'll never leave Vakovia alive, Ryan. You're as dead as me."

He laughed until he choked, and the knife in his side let the blood spill freely. In seconds, he had gone silent, and his sightless eyes stared up at the clear blue.

Shane left the narrow passage, crossed the next street, and then the one after. Two helicopters approached in the distance.

The Reapers were coming, and he had little time to escape.

EPILOGUE

Dust rose behind the SUV like smoke from a raging fire. It moved in thick, slow clouds, obscuring everything in the distance until it thinned to a faint haze. In the heat, it just made everything feel more oppressive.

The sign on the side of the road read Ulenka. It was not on any map, and didn't qualify as a town at any rate. Ulenka was a blink-and-you'll-miss-it village of no more than fifty people. A few farms, a handful of homes built around the same crossroads, and nothing more. It was a funeral that hadn't happened yet.

Carver stepped from the SUV out into the blistering sunlight. The brightness did not make him squint, and the heat did not penetrate his flesh. He had no true flesh with which to feel the heat. He was dead. Had been for the better part of sixty years.

His partner, Avery Trent, left the SUV as well. Trent had been an Army Ranger for ten years. He was a beast of a man who had briefly dabbled in powerlifting after his retirement before joining Reaper Company.

At just over six feet tall and two-hundred-and-twenty pounds, Avery cut a formidable figure. The SIG MCX-Spear rifle he carried didn't hurt the image, either. Dressed in black tactical gear with bullet-resistant body armor, a pair of Glock 19s, and a non-standard-issue hunting knife big enough to skin a rhino on his hip, he looked like death.

This was not a man who wasted time debating the moral or ethical positions that his work presented. If he needed to kill someone, he killed them. There was never a question about why or if there was a better way. He didn't care.

"Everyone dies," Trent once said when another of the Reapers asked him about it. "I shoot you today or you get hit by a bus tomorrow. Or you get brain cancer. Either way, you die. What difference does it make if I kill you myself?"

Carver appreciated that about the man. Too few of the living understood the arbitrariness of life. Why did one person live to be one hundred and then thirty kids die in a school bus crash? Why could a person who burns down hospitals live to retirement and an inspirational philanthropist die of cancer before thirty? Life and death were meaningless. Carver knew that better than most, having been both alive and dead.

Avery nodded toward the barn in the distance, about fifty yards from the road. Nothing stirred in the town, and the scant few cars looked like relics from the eighties. It was hard to imagine they worked at all.

If the people of Ulenka were home, they were hiding. Carver would find them eventually. But the barn was priority.

He had never met their target, had only seen a photo, the same as everyone else. Retired Marine, they'd said. Wanted for the murder of several Reaper Company operatives and a handful of civilians. No one said why he was in Vakovia. Hired on a contract is what Avery thought. Carver didn't care. He just wanted to kill him.

Before Reaper Company, Carver had haunted a rail yard in Michigan. He died there in nineteen sixty-six. A police bullet in the small of his back tore through his spine and killed him instantly. An inauspicious end to a life that probably could have been better lived.

He had been on the run from the cops for a robbery that turned into a double homicide. He hadn't intended to shoot anyone, but they had come out of nowhere. He killed them, he ran, he got shot. Then he came back.

Fifty-four years he haunted that same rail yard. He'd been responsible for just a few deaths in that time. Drifters, mostly, and some junkies. No more than twenty. Maybe thirty over the years. But he'd developed a taste for it. Watching the living as they realized they were dying was a thrill to him, one of the few sources of joy he could muster.

Something was revelatory there, but it had never fully manifested itself. When Carver watched death wash over a person's face, when he witnessed the exact moment their brain shut down and life ended, he felt like he almost understood something. But the moment was always too fast. He needed to keep chasing it. He wanted whatever truth was hidden there.

At some point, the ghost realized it was like a flavor for which he had no name. A taste, like a memory, of something so long forgotten it stirred the back of the mind but refused to fully open the door. But he knew if he kept trying, if he kept taking lives, he would see what he was meant to see. He would know something about what death was. So far, he'd not proven anything.

When the soldier who could see him showed up and recruited him, he almost didn't believe it. It had to be a scam. But who scams the dead? And why? He had nothing to lose, so he showed them where his haunted item was, and they took him away.

Since then, he'd traveled the world like he never had in life. He'd killed people in seven countries. It was a real thrill. He might have called it life-affirming if he were alive. But it was something. It felt right. Like he finally had a purpose. Like he'd be staring down the truth in no time.

Carver was good at killing. He could do it fast when he needed to, and quietly. He'd learned that in the train yard. Needed to be quiet there if he wanted to do it right and not be interrupted.

Sometimes, he didn't have to be fast, and he liked that, too. Sometimes, they needed answers out of people, and the dead were so much better at interrogation. A living interrogator might beat someone. They could waterboard them, electrocute them, or cut them. But Carver could do so much more.

When Carver needed answers, he could show someone their

nightmares. He could plunge a finger into their flesh and freeze their organs from the inside. He could peel muscle from bone without breaking the skin. He was very good at getting answers.

The barns in Vakovia didn't look like barns back home. No one had a red-painted barn in Vakovia. And they were never as large. The Ulenka barn he approached was natural wood; no one had bothered to weather-treat it. The panels were sun-bleached to a pale gray and warped along the ground. It was short but very long, resembling more of a warehouse than a barn.

Carver floated through the barn door and into the dark interior. Light peeked through a thousand tiny cracks but not enough in any one space to offer serious illumination. It didn't matter. Carver saw just as well in the dark.

The barn was piled with hay, big stacks of it, along the side walls. A pitchfork was buried in the nearest pile, and more tools hung on the opposite wall. Chains and hooks and scythes and sickles. It made him smile. Lots of ways to rend flesh in the barn. Lots of ways to make someone scream.

Behind him, the door pulled open on screaming, rusty hinges. Carver looked back as Avery entered the barn, scanning from left to right with his rifle drawn.

"Anything?" the living man asked.

"Not yet," the ghost replied. His voice was dry and sounded older than it had when he was alive. He didn't know why that happened when he died, but he could do nothing to change it.

The interior of the barn was split in two with a narrow half-wall in the middle. The right side was hay, and the left held tools, crates, boxes, and tables of clutter all the way to the back.

Carver chose the cluttered side. It would be easier for him to navigate. He didn't have to worry about getting around or under things, nor did he need to worry about making noise.

One of the other spectral assets had claimed this man they hunted could kill ghosts. Carver didn't believe it; the idea was absurd. But the fact the others were saying it caught his interest. It meant they were afraid. Somehow this man, this living person, had become a boogeyman for Reaper Company.

Carver and Avery had not been with the unit in Vakovia when the mission started. Their unit was in Africa, along the border of the Sudan, when they got the call that Vakovia had gone off the rails. Most of the unit had been killed by the time they arrived.

There were disturbances in the dust on the floor here and there. Not footprints, but signs things had been recently moved or jostled. Maybe someone was consciously trying to not leave tracks; Carver couldn't say. Tracking wasn't his greatest skill, so he didn't spend a lot of time analyzing.

No one was hiding in the mess. Avery would have to have tossed all the clutter, lifted tables, inspected boxes, and moved piles. All Carver had to do was walk through them and use his eyes. There was nowhere the living could hide from the dead. But there was no one hiding.

Teams had searched for the Marine for several weeks now. They knew he was in the countryside, but he was hard to pin down. The few reports that had come in were literal dead ends. The last team that reported him was found dead fifty miles to the south. The SEAL's neck was broken, and his spectral asset was missing.

Carver didn't doubt the man was dangerous, but he was no boogeyman. Reaper Company had an ego problem; he'd seen that the day he joined up. Soldiers paired with ghosts started to think they were unstoppable after a while. The dead did most of the work, but the living got the credit, and that made them smug. They got more and more money and more and more impossible jobs. And every success made Reaper Company's reputation grow. They could do anything.

If a few soldiers got sloppy, believed their hype, and then died as a result, that was Reapers reaping what they sowed, as far as Carver was concerned. He couldn't be like that, and he knew Avery wouldn't, either. Avery was a simple man with simple needs. He barely talked, he did the job, and he went home.

Carver reached the end of the barn and found nothing. There was no sign of the target, or that he had been there.

"Clear," he shouted. There was no response from Avery.

The ghost crossed over to the side of the barn piled with haystacks and looked back toward the entrance. He could not see his partner.

"Avery," Carver shouted again. "Avery, we're all clear here. Where are you?"

In the years they had worked together, Avery had been nothing but efficient. He didn't wander off, and he didn't go off task.

Hay rustled in his wake as Carver rushed toward the front of the barn. He had heard nothing. If the target had shown up, even if he had somehow disarmed Avery, there would have been a struggle, some sign to alert him.

Carver returned to the barn's entrance and stopped next to the first pile. The barn door was still open, held in place by Avery's body. He was face-down on the ground, the pitchfork from the hay pile pierced through the back of his neck.

The ghost was silent. He pried the body of his partner off the ground, lifting the tines of the fork that pinned him in place, and flipped the body over. The barn hinges screamed as the door began to slowly swing shut. Carver stared down at Avery's face. His eyes were open, and blood still flowed from the wounds in his neck.

The barn door closed with a thunk. Carver looked up at it, his eyes widening.

BEHIND YOU

The message was scrawled hastily on the barn door. It was written in blood.

Carver turned quickly and saw nothing. The hay sat still and silent like the rest of the barn.

"You're going to die!" the ghost shouted into the seemingly empty building. He turned to look at the door again. The sound of soft rustling filled the emptiness.

Carver turned back as hay fell away from the pile. A dark figure rose from the center, his face and clothing smeared with mud and clay-like slashes of discolored shadow and light, camouflaging him in the darkened barn.

"It's you," Carver hissed. The man they had been looking for.

The boogeyman of Reaper Company. Shane Ryan.

"It is," Ryan agreed in a whisper. He leaped from the hay and Carver barely had time to register surprise as the man's hands hit him but did not pass through. He held him as though he were still alive, still had a physical body, and threw him to the ground.

"H-how—?"

It was the only word he could force out. Ryan's hand pushed into his mouth, and he felt the man's muscles tense. Carver screamed, not from pain but fear, as he felt his form responding. He was not flesh anymore, not alive anymore, and none of it should have been possible.

He heard his lower jaw crack inside his head before it pulled away. Ryan's other hand was pressing down hard. Carver bucked and writhed under the man's weight. The ghost felt the living man's weight. He was heavy and solid and impossible to move. It couldn't have been real.

He screamed again, the sound of an animal caught in a trap. He knew it was coming. He could feel it as sure as he could feel the pressure building in his skull. Shane Ryan could kill the dead, and he was going to kill Carver.

There was one final crunch, and everything went black. In that last moment, Carver laughed.

There was no truth in death. He had learned nothing.

Check out these best-selling series from our talented authors:

GHOST STORIES

RON RIPLEY

BERKLEY STREET SERIES
MOVING IN SERIES
HAUNTED COLLECTION SERIES
DEATH HUNTER SERIES

IAN FORTEY

JIGSAW OF SOULS SERIES
CULT OF THE ENDLESS NIGHT SERIES

SUPERNATURAL SUSPENSE

A. I. NASSER

SLAUGHTER SERIES
SIN SERIES

DAVID LONGHORN

NIGHTMARE SERIES
ASYLUM SERIES

SARA CLANCY

THE BELL WITCH SERIES
BANSHEE SERIES

For a complete list of our new releases and best-selling horror books, visit
ScareStreet.com or scan the QR code below!